NANCY HOLLAND

Born in California (and always a California girl at heart), I'm now a teacher in the Upper Midwest. I wrote my first novel at the age of seven – a saga about a family of chipmunks and the family of ducks who lived in the pond next door. I've been writing ever since.

My husband and I are lucky enough to have two smart, wonderful children who live on opposite coasts of the US. Since I've become a HarperImpulse author, my remaining daydream is to live in Paris or London.

www.nancyhollandwriter.com

@NancyHolland5

Owed: One Wedding Night

NANCY HOLLAND

Harper*Impulse* an imprint of
HarperCollins*Publishers* Ltd
1 London Bridge Street
London SE1 9GF

www.harpercollins.co.uk

A Paperback Original 2015

First published in Great Britain in ebook format by Harper*Impulse* 2015

A catalogue record for this book is
available from the British Library

ISBN: 9780008149482

couldn't make it. I'm her daughter."

The redhead gave a small shrug and pushed a hidden button on the desk.

"Your ten o'clock appointment is here, Mr. Carlyle."

The distance from the reception area to Jake Carlyle's office was only a fraction of the walk from the elevator, but it felt ten times longer. At every clack of Madison's heels on polished marble, the urge to forget this whole plan and head for the safety of home threatened to overwhelm her.

She forced her mother's worried face to the front of her mind to block out everything but her promise to save Dartmoor Department Stores. If she thought too much about how Jake might react when he saw her, she could never do this. But her mother had paid too high a price to hold on to the family business for Madison to quit now.

Besides, there was no reason she and the head of Carlyle & Sons couldn't discuss the issue like adults.

The receptionist glided ahead of her and opened the door to the office with a flourish.

The antique mahogany desk that dominated the room on the other side of the door was impressive. The man behind it was even more impressive.

Jake Carlyle's face was elevated above mere masculine good looks by the slash of cheekbones inherited from the fashion model who had deigned to become his mother. The hand-tailored gray pinstripe suit emphasized the power of his tall, muscular frame.

He stood with a frown as Madison stepped into his inner sanctum.

Merely looking at the man took her breath away. When he raised sapphire-blue eyes to meet hers, her heart stopped entirely, then thudded back to life in double time.

Taking him by surprise was the only point in her favor. She watched the emotions run across the face she knew so well – surprise, a hint of lust, curiosity, and, finally, the beginnings of anger.

2

Chapter One

Madison Ellsworth's heart pounded in rhythm with the noisy staccato of her heels on the marble floor of Carlyle & Sons' San Francisco headquarters. The unwelcoming glass-and-steel decor, softened only here and there by hand-woven wall-hangings in shades of rust, gold, and azure, made the long path from the elevator to the receptionist's desk seem endless.

She could do this. She had to do this. Her mother had gone through so much in the last two months. The least Madison could do was take this one burden off of her shoulders. If she felt like a sacrificial lamb on the way to slaughter, she had no one to blame but herself. She crossed her fingers for luck.

When she finally reached the stunning metal sculpture that was the receptionist's desk, the redhead who sat behind it looked up at her with a small frown.

Madison shifted the Italian leather briefcase her mother had given her when she got into Stanford Business School from one damp hand to the other. "I'm here to see Mr. Carlyle."

"I'm sorry." The receptionist didn't sound sorry at all. "He has an appointment with," she glanced at the computer screen, cleverly hidden in the desk. "With a Mrs. Ellsworth."

Madison took a deep breath and resisted the need to lift a hand and check that her sleek up-do was still perfect. "Mrs. Ellsworth

In loving memory of my mother, who introduced me to romance and always believed this day would come.

The anger made him lift his head slightly. His expression returned to the polite boredom a man like Jake Carlyle displayed to mere mortals, yet a frisson of sexual excitement lingered in the climate-controlled air.

"What are you doing here?"

Just what her frayed nerves needed – the man was channeling her father. She took a deep breath to calm herself.

"Mother doesn't feel well, so I came instead."

He looked away. For a moment, she'd rattled him. She lifted her chin a little higher and waited for his next move.

"How is she? It must have been a terrible shock."

Madison's eyes stung with a rush of unexpected grief. Shock, yes. Terrible, yes. But not in the way he thought.

For a moment the devastating memory of that pre-dawn phone call, made stronger by being in Jake's presence, threatened to overwhelm her. Her first impulse, almost a compulsion, had been to call him, to go to him for the strength and comfort she needed, even though she'd no longer had a right to expect anything from him. Reality, and duty, had won out. She'd gone to her mother, been the strong one, the comforter. She'd had no other choice.

She fought off the still raw pain by making the Ms.-Manners-approved response. "It was nice of you to come to my father's memorial service."

"Old friends and all that. You and your parents came to the one for my father."

Those two unhappy events were the only times she and Jake had seen each other in three years. She sighed.

The momentary weakness didn't go unpunished.

"So why did you, or rather your mother, want to talk to me?"

The ice in his voice made her knees wobble. Obviously the pleasantries were over.

She gave a meaningful look at the comfortable chairs that flanked the fireplace at the far end of the office, but instead he gestured at the stiff leather chair across the desk from his. They sat down at the same moment, eyes fixed on each other's faces, like boxers circling in the ring.

She took a deep breath and began in a professional tone she hoped she could hang on to. "How much do you know about the circumstances surrounding my father's death?"

He had the good grace to look uncomfortable. "Only what was in the newspapers. I didn't follow all the stuff that showed up on the web."

And thank you for that.

"I take it there are financial issues," he continued.

She wondered if that was how her mother had phrased it when she made this appointment. Or was he only being polite? Madison took another deep breath and carefully unknotted her hands.

"These last few years. . ." She forced air into her lungs. "My father's relationship with Dartmoor's Chief Financial Officer. . ." Anger and shame, added to the nervousness that kept her heart pounding double time, finally stole her voice.

Jake chose to be merciful. "The woman he was with when he died?"

She nodded. Able to breathe again, she gave up on spontaneity as a bad bet and launched into the speech her mother would have made.

"Dartmoor Department Stores has suffered from an unfortunate lack of financial oversight recently that has left it in a difficult situation. New leadership. . ." Her heart stumbled at the thought. "New leadership is now in place."

At least she'd been able to convince her father's mistress to resign. Firing her would only have added to the scandal. Unfortunately, nothing could be done about the all-cash golden parachute the former CFO and Madison's father had set up for her, which had decimated Dartmoor's cash reserves.

"However," Madison continued, "the missteps of the previous CFO have left the company seriously short of the capital it needs to move forward in this challenging economy."

"Missteps, incompetence, or fraud?" Jake interrupted.

Madison looked down. "We're not sure."

"Has the new leadership you referred to had a forensic audit done?"

Her face heated. "That would cost more money than seemed wise to spend on the chance it would turn up any criminal misconduct."

Criminal misconduct, which might, she didn't bother to add, implicate her father.

She raised her eyes to search Jake's face for some clue as to what he might be thinking, but met only a stare so cold it knocked what she meant to say next out of her mind completely.

"Go on," he said. "I didn't mean to interrupt such a carefully canned speech."

His disdain shook her mind free of its temporary paralysis. "Unfortunately, most of my mother's assets and those of the other investors in Dartmoor have also been victims of the economy, and as things stand there's little chance of attracting private capital or new investors."

"What about the trust fund from your grandmother?"

Of course he'd remember that little detail.

"My mother and I have been living on it since my father died." Nana's money had also put Madison through business school, but she didn't dare say so. "We're spending the principal now." She suppressed a shudder at the thought of how soon they'd use up the last of that.

Jake shook his head. She was probably the only person in the world beside his mother who would recognize the tiny tic of impatience at one corner of his mouth.

His voice was as bland as his features. "So, where do I come into the picture?"

She looked past him out the window at the sunshine glinting off the building across the street. No inspiration there.

If it was up to her, she'd have sold everything and lived in a tent in Golden Gate Park rather than answer Jake's question. She'd exhausted every other option first. She'd sold the condo where she lived while she was in business school and now shared the Pacific Heights apartment her mother had moved into when she'd been forced to sell their home in Marin County.

Jake sat there, watching her.

Panic swept over her, choked her. She couldn't do this. There had to be another way. She'd let Dartmoor go and take one of the jobs she'd been offered in Silicon Valley. She and her mother could get an apartment together down there. . .

And her mother would be miserable. The humiliation of having her husband die in another woman's bed, then all the stress of learning that they might have to close Dartmoor had already aged Dana Ellsworth ten years in the last two months. She'd had lived a mockery of a marriage for as long as Madison could remember and even that might not have been enough to keep Dartmoor in the family.

Which is why Madison was sitting here, face hot with humiliation, damp hands once again knotted in her lap.

She let out a long, slow breath. "If you would loan my mother. . ." She couldn't finish.

He raised his eyebrows in a way she'd once thought the sexiest thing in the world. Right now the gesture made her look for a waste basket, in case her stomach betrayed her completely.

"How much?"

She named a figure that made Jake's eyes open wide.

"How much of that is for Dartmoor and how much is to support your mother's lifestyle? Not to mention yours?"

Madison was tempted to tell him her lifestyle, as bare-bones as it had become lately, was none of his business. But that wouldn't help her mother.

"All the money will be used to implement my plan to revitalize Dartmoor."

Both his eyebrows went up. "Your plan?"

This was the opening she needed. She lifted the briefcase to her lap and opened it.

"Yes. If you look at the some of my ideas, you'll see. . ."

He held up his hand. "Spare me. I don't think I can sit through another of your amateur sales pitches."

She started to protest that her MBA in marketing made her far from an amateur, but the look on his face, somewhere between amusement and rage, stopped her. Instead she set the case down again and tried to ignore the memories that kept flooding back and threatened to make it impossible for her to continue.

"So, the money would all go to Dartmoor."

She nodded.

"And what will you two live on in the meantime?"

What should she tell him? The whole truth wasn't an option.

"I've had several job offers."

Something dark crossed his face, then evaporated.

"Jobs that will pay enough to support your mother's current lifestyle?"

"No." That was true enough. "But with my trust fund, we'll manage."

He leaned forward in his chair, arms on the desk. With an effort she managed not to draw back, away from the masculine energy of his body.

"And how to you plan to pay back this loan? Out of Dartmoor's profits? Unlikely, any time soon. Out of your salary? I don't think so."

"Jake, I have a photo of you at my christening." He flinched, probably at the image of himself as a bored, but adorable four-year-old in a stiff black suit. "If you loan us the money, you know I'll pay you back, no matter what happens."

"I doubt either of us will live long enough for you to pay me back that kind of money out of your paychecks."

Somehow Jake must have missed the news that she'd finished her MBA at the top of her class. She sat up a little straighter. She might not have made much in the short term if she'd taken any of those jobs, but in a year, ten years, she'd have been earning the money to pay him back several times over. A man as smart as he was could figure that out. Maybe he wasn't ready to accept that he'd been wrong when he tried to veto her plan to go to business school.

The impulse to run away that had lurked at the back of her mind ever since she entered the building took over. She set both feet on the floor, ready to stand up, when she remembered that this time it wasn't about her. It was about her mother and saving the family legacy.

She sat back and crossed her legs. If she had to stay, the best defense might be a good offense.

"If you're worried I might stiff you for the money by dying, I could take out a life- insurance policy for the full amount and make you the beneficiary. If I pay you back most of it and something happens to me, you'd make a nice profit on the deal."

He scowled. "That's not the point. The point is that a loan implies an ability to repay the money. Frankly, I can't see how that's supposed to happen. Maybe your MBA will take you right to the executive suite." She flinched, but he didn't notice. "Or maybe you'll get laid off or have an employer fail on you, and then where would I be?"

"Still filthy rich." Not exactly the right attitude when she was asking him for such a big favor, but the man knew how to push her buttons. All of them.

"So you want me to give you the money for old times' sake?" He leaned back in his chair and looked her straight in the eye.

She shook off the shattering impact of his gaze, impatient at her inability to keep the past behind her.

Apparently he couldn't forget what they'd shared either. But she couldn't believe he'd refuse to help because their wedding plans had fallen through. That didn't sound like the Jake she'd once adored. She searched for that Jake in the face of the stranger in front of her.

8

"Is that what you would have said if it was my mother sitting here?"

"Not in those words, no, but whatever I said to her would have led to the same outcome – no loan."

"What about half that amount?" It was better than nothing.

He shook his head.

The clang of a cable-car bell found its way up from the street below. She took a calming breath against the anger that simmered just below the surface.

"I expected better of you, Jake. I expected you to at least look at my plan to turn Dartmoor around."

"Because?"

"Because you're a fair man. And you know I will repay you, no matter what."

He shrugged and picked up a pen from his desk with a this-conversation-is-over gesture.

"I think we all learned a long time ago that I am the last person to predict what you will or will not do."

She leaned forward, hands on the edge of his desk. "I'm not asking you to do this for me." No power on earth could make her stoop that low. "I'm asking you to do it for my mother."

"I won't be doing it at all. I was always fond of your mother, but this is business."

She sank back. She wasn't sure what she'd expected from Jake, but certainly more than that icy dismissal. When he didn't say anything more, she reluctantly gathered her purse and briefcase to leave, mind already searching for other ways to get the money.

She was halfway out of the chair when he said, "Madison."

She sat back down and lifted her head.

"Tell your mother I'm sorry."

"I'm sure she'll find that a great comfort when they liquidate her family business because you refused to help."

His eyes narrowed as he stood. "You never do know when to shut up, do you?"

9

Anger propelled her to her feet. She would not let him loom over her like a predator over its prey.

"Maybe not, but I do know refusing to marry you was the smartest thing I ever did."

On that blatant lie, she turned to walk out.

"Madi." The old nickname came unwanted to Jake's lips. He couldn't let her go. Not with those words hanging in the air between them.

She turned. Hope battled with wariness in her sea-green eyes as she waited for him to say something. But what?

He needed time to think. To adjust to having her so close he could smell her perfume – the same exotic French scent he remembered, full of unspoken promises. So close he could see the little worry line between her eyes, could touch her. . .

"Dinner," he said.

She frowned.

"I don't have time to listen to your plan now. Let's have dinner tonight. I can look at what you've come up with then and decide whether it can turn Dartmoor around and make a loan viable."

A glow lit up her face.

"I'm not making any promises." He just wasn't ready to let her walk out of his life again.

The light in her eyes dimmed. "Of course not."

"The Yacht Club?" His turf – and the opposite of romantic.

"Sure. What time?"

"Seven." That would give him time to have a drink in the bar first. He'd need it. "Do you want me to send the limo for you?"

"No."

He thought he heard an echo of disappointment in her voice. She couldn't have expected him to pick her up. This wasn't a date. It was strictly business. Suuuure it was.

"I haven't had to sell the Ferrari yet."

Her sad smile twisted his heart.

"Oh." He'd refused to let her return his engagement gift after the wedding fell through. What would he have done with the damned car? And she loved it so much.

Her smile faded as they stared at each other for a moment too long. Long enough for the good memories to outnumber the bad. For him, at least.

Luckily his cell buzzed noisily before he could do or say anything stupid.

"I'll see you tonight." Her voice told him nothing.

He nodded and took his call, all too aware of the door closing behind her as she left.

He couldn't settle down to work after he ended the call. He walked to the windows and gazed down at the busy parade of people on Montgomery Street, the heart of the San Francisco financial district, several floors below. His father had preferred the office next door overlooking San Francisco Bay, but Jake had switched his office with the boardroom when he took over Carlyle's. The Bay was his father's escape, an escape that eventually proved fatal and made Jake President and Chair of the Board before he was thirty.

The darkness of those days lingered. The tinge of Madison's perfume that hung in the air was an aching reminder of how he'd longed to have her comfort and strength beside him through it all. But she'd made her choice. She'd chosen business school and left him at the altar.

Which is why Jake preferred Montgomery Street. It put the past behind him, where it belonged. The energy of the busy street below recharged him, motivated him, drove him. He needed all that and more after the scene with Madison.

When she first walked in – dark circles under her eyes expensive make-up couldn't hide, pale-blonde hair twisted up on her head, wearing the same black suit she'd worn to her father's funeral – he'd been stunned by the double whammy of tension in his gut and a pang in his heart. But before he could decide whether to take her in his arms or start raging about what she'd done to him, he realized how nervous she was. That one moment of sympathy had earned him twenty minutes of feigning the cold indifference toward her he wished he felt.

He'd avoided her for the last three years because he knew seeing her again would turn him inside out like this. A need that was far more than physical still gnawed at his gut.

Every time she'd traded verbal jabs with him the way she used to, his libido had jumped into overdrive. It had been all he could do not to grab her and take her in every way a man could.

Madison had always had that effect on him. Erotic memories flooded his mind, hardened his body, before he could stop them.

He banished them in an instant with the memory of standing at the church door, where her father had told him in a red-faced rage, "The little bitch isn't coming. She says she's sorry. Sorry! After all the money I threw away on this fiasco."

Then her father had taken Jake's arm, dragged him to the altar, and made him stand there while the preacher announced to the hundreds of people in attendance that the wedding was off.

Now Madison expected Jake to loan her mother money because he was "a fair man". She'd been pushing the limits to expect him not to throw her bodily out of his office the minute she appeared in the door.

So why ask her out to dinner? He had no intention of loaning her, or her mother, a penny. And he certainly had no intention of letting her flaunt her plan – a product of the MBA, which had been so much more important to her than he was – over dinner.

She'd hurt him so badly the scars hadn't completely healed three years later. The impulse to hurt her back pounded through his brain, but he wasn't that kind of man.

No, he hadn't asked her to dinner to get his revenge. He'd done it simply because the idea of not seeing her again was more than he could bear.

Madison's hands were shaking so hard she could barely get the key into the ignition of the beloved vintage Ferrari that was the last remaining sign Jake Carlyle had once loved her.

If you could call it love when he couldn't understand why she wanted to get the education she'd need to build a career at Dartmoor, the way he had at Carlyle & Sons.

In any case, love surely was not the reason behind his dinner invitation. A sincere concern for her mother's welfare, if not her own, maybe.

Or simple lust. As if she'd hop back into his bed after everything that had happened.

She started to hand the parking attendant a credit card before she remembered her new rules and pulled a ten out of her wallet instead. The car behind her honked at the delay.

She took her time collecting her change before she drove on, then refocused on Jake's dinner invitation. She didn't know what he had in mind, but she did know how angry he'd been when she didn't show up for the wedding. And how humiliated. Her father had described it all in great detail, along with his own disgust, before he'd cut her out of his life for good.

Jake was probably out for revenge, and yet she'd said yes. The remote possibility that he might loan them the money had only been part of it. An hour or two with the only man she'd ever loved, with or without the loan, had for one weak moment seemed worth whatever revenge he planned to take. Besides, what horrible things could he say to her that she hadn't already said to herself a hundred times?

Maybe once she survived this dinner and he'd had his revenge, she could forgive herself and get on with her life. Still, the prospect of life without Jake had never looked more bleak.

Chapter Two

"Ms. Ellsworth." The maître d' at the Yacht Club greeted Madison with genuine warmth. "It's been quite a while since you graced us with your presence."

Three years, to be precise. After the non-wedding, she'd stayed away for fear she might run into her father, until he'd given up his membership and sold the yacht. Then she hadn't had any reason to come here at all.

"It's nice to see you again, too, Marcel. I'm here to meet Jake Carlyle."

Marcel was a true professional. The only sign of surprise was a momentary widening of his eyes. "Of course, Ms. Ellsworth. I'll let him know you're here."

None of the people who passed through the lobby in a range of attire from swimsuits to thousand-dollar business suits gave her a second glance. Apparently she'd struck the right fashion note for dinner with her ex-fiancé – a navy-blue silk dress with pearls and dressy black sandals that matched the large purse holding her tablet computer. Business-like but feminine.

And this was just business, of course. Either the literal business of the loan Dartmoor so desperately needed or, more likely, the business of letting Jake have his moment of revenge.

The Yacht Club was the perfect place for it. Everyone they

knew would either be in the building or hear about it the next day from someone who was. Strategic planning had always been Jake's strong suit.

"Madi."

Another clever strategy. He'd thrown her off-balance by appearing from the deck behind her rather than from the bar. She turned to face him.

Dear lord, the man was gorgeous. Shirt open at the neck, hair tousled by the wind, blue eyes crinkled against the brightly lit space – he was every woman's dream. Her dream.

And her nightmare. Walking away from this man was the hardest thing she'd ever done. The hole it left inside her still bled at odd moments. Now, for instance. She could only stare at him while he waited for a simple greeting she couldn't quite muster.

He smiled, but not the smug smile she half expected, one that showed he was well aware of the effect he had on her. No, he smiled at her as if seeing her made him happy, as if she brought the kind of joy into his life he used to bring into hers.

She might have stood there forever if Marcel hadn't reappeared with a bow and led them to a secluded table in the dining room that overlooked the rippling waters of the bay.

She endured the stares and mutters of the people they passed, used to living with the scandal her father had created. Thankfully Jake didn't act as if he noticed any of it.

"Do you get out to sail often?" she asked, for lack of anything else to say once the server had taken their drink orders.

A potent mixture of grief and anger crossed his face. "I don't sail anymore at all."

She'd forgotten. His father had died sailing alone on the bay. "I'm sorry."

"I won't say it gets easier, but you do learn to live with the loss."

"I'll take your word for it."

She could imagine learning to live with her father's death. It was what he'd done while he was alive that she found so hard to forget – or forgive. Probably because she was still living with the consequences, including this awkward dinner.

Jake reached across the table to take the hand she'd unconsciously extended toward him, as if to comfort him. His face took on the same look of intense interest as before, as if she were the only thing in the world that mattered. She wished.

He lifted her hand to his lips with the quirk of a smile.

"But let's not dwell on the past. Any of it."

She jerked free of the 110-volt charge that shot through her system, expecting to see scorch marks on her hand.

To hide the heat that colored her face, she picked up her purse from the floor by her side.

"Maybe we can discuss my plan for Dartmoor over drinks."

His lips tightened before he smiled again. "I'd rather spend some time getting to know each other again first. How's your mother doing?"

He kept up a steady flow of small talk masquerading as real conversation through their drinks, salad, and entrée. Every time she tried to shift the topic back to Dartmoor, he came up with some new question she couldn't find a way to dodge.

After a while she stopped trying. Clearly the whole evening was a sham. He had no interest in her plan. He'd brought her here for revenge, pure and simple.

Which replaced nervousness about showing him her plan with a deeper anxiety about what he intended to do, and when.

The few bites of salad Niçoise she'd managed to eat were followed by even fewer bites of steamed mussels and garlic-mashed potatoes. The tension that left less and less room in her stomach for food also pushed all the air out of her lungs, so the polite chitchat became almost impossible.

"Dessert?"

She shook her head.

"Here, have some more wine."

This was the third time he'd asked and she'd said no. Or was it the fourth? She put a hand over her glass. "I'm driving."

His polite smile widened and something she didn't trust twinkled in his eyes.

"I could give you a ride home."

Anger restored the backbone that had been melting away all evening. She lifted her head to meet his vaguely mocking gaze.

"I'm not a member here anymore. If I leave my car in the lot overnight, they'll have it towed in a nanosecond."

He hesitated for a moment, as if he hadn't quite decided whether to try to seduce her or not, then he set the wine bottle down and took the last bite of his steak.

She let out the breath she'd been holding, not a hundred percent certain she could resist a seduction, if he tried. Her defenses, never strong when it came to Jake, were way down after an evening spent watching his face, his sensual enjoyment of the food, the way his hands moved. An evening of remembering and storing up new memories for a future without him. Her whole body ached and burned with a desire that could only destroy her.

Maybe that was his revenge.

"So," he asked casually as he finished his wine, "what poor fool did the Dartmoor Board convince to take over as their CEO?"

She swallowed a cry of pain as the blood drained from her face.

He couldn't know, but this would be his true revenge. Not only had he refused to listen to her plan to save Dartmoor, now she'd have to reveal the one fact guaranteed to keep him from ever loaning them the money they needed. No reason to put off the inevitable.

"Me."

He gave his head a little shake. "I beg your pardon?"

"They convinced me to take over as acting CEO."

Jake understood the words one by one, but together they made no sense. He could imagine Madi as a management trainee, but CEO, even acting CEO of a multi-million-dollar corporation? No way. He decided to play along.

"You always said you wanted to be head of Dartmoor someday."

She gave him a grim smile. "The operative word being someday. I fought them pretty hard, actually."

Damn, it was true. A probably irrational anger burned through him.

"Why didn't you just go for it? I mean, you got your MBA a whole four months ago. What else would you need to run an operation the size of Dartmoor?"

Her posture stiffened as she lifted her head to match his gaze full on.

"I don't run Dartmoor. I replaced my father, who hardly ever went into the office except to do the deed with his mistress. After he created the position of Chief Operating Officer, my father reduced the CEO's role to vision, strategic planning, and hanging out at the club with the other old boys."

He couldn't suppress a grin at the image of her fulfilling that last role.

"So, your plan to fix Dartmoor is the official one?"

"It's in the developmental stage. I didn't want to get anyone's hopes up." Her posture went more rigid. "Which is a good thing, since I can't get the one person I was sure we could count on for a loan to even look at the plan."

She'd counted on him? Jake didn't know how to feel about that. More anger was safest.

"You gave up any right to guilt-trip me when you left me at the altar, Madi."

Her body seemed to melt in front of him like a candle set too close to a fire.

"You're right. I only. . ." She sniffed. "My mother. . ."

He missed the warrior woman, but had no clue how to get her back. "I'm sorry."

No, that sounded like an apology for what he said, but he'd meant it.

18

"I'm sorry your father was a jerk. I'm sorry he died. But I can't loan you money I don't think you can repay. If Dartmoor's in as serious trouble as you say it is, no matter how much money you make as acting CEO, you won't be making it for long."

She gave a low laugh. "Real-life business lesson number one – never make a deal without doing your due diligence. When I took the job, I agreed to greatly reduced compensation from Dartmoor as a signal to our employees that I was serious about straightening out our financial problems. Then I learned how bad they were. My salary doesn't even pay the rent. What I told you this afternoon is true. Mother and I are living on the principal of my trust fund."

He resisted the need to touch her hand. "I wish I knew a way. . ."

A tiny spark lit in her eyes. "There is a way." She reached down for her purse.

"No, Madi. There isn't. But I am sorry."

He was definitely a sorry person tonight. But what else could he say?

She carefully set her napkin on the table and started to stand. "In that case, maybe I should go."

He reached out and took her wrist. "Don't leave."

For one moment her face softened before it hardened again and she glared at his hand.

"Let me walk you to your car," he said.

Slowly she nodded and he let go.

He kept one eye on her while he signed for dinner. Twice she made a move as if to walk away, but both times their eyes met and she stayed. At least some of the old magic still worked.

He escorted her out of the dining room, ignoring the stares of people who remembered, or had heard, about their past together.

When they stepped out into the foggy night, he didn't ask where she was parked, but took the path that ran along the water. Again she moved to pull away, but when he took hold of the sleeve of her jacket, she fell into step with him.

Out of habit he led her to the empty slip he'd held onto in

19

case someday he could bear to sail the Bay again. He stopped and rested his elbows on the weathered wooden gate, one foot raised to the bottom rail. Beside him, Madison stared over at the next dock, at her family's old slip and the yacht that her Grandfather Moore had had built fifty years ago and named after her mother. The "Dana Marie" was now the "Blue Sky".

The mist had curled the hair around Madison's face. Her eyes were wide and wistful, like a poor kid peering into a toy-store window at Christmas. Not because she wanted the yacht back. She'd always been more interested in sunbathing on the deck than sailing. No, she had to want her old life back.

Something sharp wrapped itself around his heart, but he willed it away.

He hadn't taken that life away from her. Her father had.

Jake hadn't taken anything away from her. She was the one who'd walked out on him, hurt him, humiliated him. . .

She must have felt him watching her, because she turned to look at him. But the wistful, wanting expression on her face didn't go away. Instead it grew darker, hotter.

A foghorn sounded. Somewhere a buoy bell clanged on the waves. A car drove by, leaving a trail of loud music in its wake.

"What happened, Madi?"

The question seemed to surprise her as much as it surprised him. She didn't answer, but stared past him toward the water.

"What happened to us?" he asked again.

"I couldn't be your trophy wife."

What the hell did that mean?

He kept his tone calm. "That's a pretty dated term. Aren't trophy wives young second wives for old guys?"

"Not necessarily. A lot of people would say, have said, our mothers were trophy wives, even though they were first wives and our fathers were only a few years older than they were."

He didn't try to deny it.

"Your father used his family's wealth to win the model of

the year as his wife," she went on. "My father won Dartmoor by marrying my mother. I'm not sure which one was the trophy there, but you get the idea."

The bitterness in her voice stunned him, but he knew her better than to comment on it.

"Even if that kind of marriage was good enough for our mothers, it would never have been enough for me, Jake. I wanted to do more with my life than have babies, hand them over to a nanny, and wait for you to come home at the end of the day."

He swallowed the sucker punch she didn't realize she'd so expertly delivered. He couldn't count how many times he'd day-dreamed about exactly that.

"We could have worked it out."

"I tried to talk with you about it. The only conversation we had about it ended with you forbidding. . ." She paused to underscore the word. "Forbidding me to get my MBA."

He remembered that argument. He'd been so angry and hurt to learn that Madison didn't wanted their marriage, their family, to be the center of her life that he hadn't known what else to say. He'd ended up silencing her outrage with a soul-searing kiss. They hadn't come up for air until the next morning.

"Your father agreed with me."

She winced.

"And you didn't bring it up again." His tone was harsher, colder than he intended.

"The wedding was a run-away train. I didn't know how to slow it down so we could talk. Our mothers had every minute scheduled for weeks. You and I were almost never alone together, and when we were we always ended up in bed. I didn't want to fight with you in bed. I kept trying to find another chance to talk to you, to work it out, but that chance never came."

Anger tightened his voice. "So you decided the best solution was to call your father from the limo on the way to the church and tell him the wedding was off."

21

"That's not what happened."

Madison took a deep, shuddering breath.

He was waiting for her to say more. The harsh parking lot lights transformed his handsome face into a demon's mask of pale skin and dark shadows.

"I called my father to tell him we were caught in traffic and would be a few minutes late."

Still no reaction from him, as if he didn't care about what had happened. Maybe, after all this time, it no longer mattered to him. But it mattered to her. She needed to tell him for her own sake, if nothing else.

"When my father answered, I heard you in the background talking to someone. Your cousin Mark, probably. You were bragging to him that I was the ultimate trophy wife. I–I couldn't go through with the wedding after that. I refused to stop being who I was, to give up my dreams to be your trophy wife, no matter how much I loved you."

His face remained frozen.

"I didn't think of you as a trophy wife."

"I heard you, Jake."

"You didn't hear the whole conversation."

He put his hands on her shoulders, but she shook herself free, wishing there was some way to stop time right there.

For three years she'd told herself, if only in her weakest moments, that maybe she'd been wrong, maybe there'd been some other explanation for what Jake said. How could she live with the guilt if she *had* been wrong? And if she hadn't, how could she live without that one tiny hope? That was why she'd never had this conversation with him. Not that he'd ever given her the chance before.

She held her breath, dreading the inevitable pain, no matter which way he answered.

He gave her a grim smile. "Mark and I were joking with each

22

other about our 'trophy wives'. He was married to a hot young starlet at the time, remember?"

"You sounded plenty serious when you said it."

He didn't say anything right away, but jammed his hands in his pocket and turned half away from her. The hesitation, the way he couldn't meet her eyes told her it would be worse than she'd feared. Whatever he said next would be a lie.

"I was serious. I didn't want him to think I really felt that way about you. I told him you were the ultimate trophy wife because you were so smart as well as beautiful."

She closed her eyes against the hurt that seemed to cut her open from neck to belly.

"Don't lie to me, Jake. Not about this."

She had to stop to breathe. She slowly counted to ten, waiting for him to say something.

He stood silent, the demon's mask back in place.

So she turned and walked away.

A gust of wind stirred the fog. Jake saw Madison shiver and automatically took the two steps to catch up with her to put his arm around her shoulder. She froze for a moment, but let him walk beside her as she crossed the parking lot to her car.

When they reach the bright-red Ferrari she shook herself free and pulled the key from her purse without the usual female rummaging around. She unlocked the door and threw her over-sized purse across to the passenger seat before she straightened and faced him.

"Good-bye, Jake. Thank you for dinner."

He couldn't find words. She climbed into the car and he swung the door shut, then watched while she started the engine and drove off.

He still hadn't moved when she pulled out of the parking lot and into the busy late-night traffic on Marina Boulevard.

Why hadn't he told her the truth about what he'd said to Mark?

He sighed and headed for his car.

Because he refused to open old wounds, refused to be that guy again. The guy who'd loved Madison so completely she'd almost destroyed him.

A trophy wife! He shook his head and got into his car.

Sure, he hadn't wanted her to get her MBA. He knew how much time and energy business school took. He'd wanted, needed, her at his side instead while he took over more and more of the day-to-day leadership at Carlyle & Sons to conceal his father's deepening depression.

He'd had to keep his business problems secret from Madison back then, for fear she'd let something slip to her jerk of a father, who would gleefully spread the news in the business community. But Jake had planned to explain the situation on their honeymoon.

The honeymoon that never happened.

As he turned his car onto Marina Boulevard, the cell he'd left in its hands-free station buzzed. He flicked it on, not caring who was calling. Even a telemarketer would be better company than a mind full of memories and regrets.

"Ah, hello, Mother," he said.

As soon as rush hour was over the next day Madison drove the Ferrari out to the newest Dartmoor store in Antioch. She needed the driving time to think about some changes in her plan, and fewer people would recognize her at this store than at those closer in, so she'd have a chance to pretend to be a shopper for a while.

Her first impression when she stepped into the store was sameness. Not sameness with the older Dartmoor stores, which varied in layout according to the age of the buildings, but sameness with every other store built the same decade in every other mall she'd ever been in. This was their most profitable store, but it lacked the distinctively Dartmoor flavor that would make shoppers look for their ads or lead them to their website.

She didn't dare take photos, but she could make a few quick

sketches of the possibilities taking shape in her mind when she got back to the car.

She started circling the first floor to get a customer's-eye view, but she couldn't see the merchandise first of all, the way a shopper would. She saw people. A seasoned professional behind the cosmetics counter giving advice to her college-age coworker. The woman ending her shift in handbags to be home to meet her kindergartner's school bus. The older woman in candy who'd worked for years at the flagship store before she moved out here to be near her grandkids. And, when the older woman recognized Madison and called upstairs, the manager who'd built her career working for Dartmoor.

The manager greeted Madison with a smile, panic in her eyes, and an outstretched hand.

"What a pleasant surprise. We're honored to have you here, Ms. Ellsworth."

The words twisted in Madison's heart. How much was honor that came from wealth and name alone worth? Especially when the next time Madison saw the woman it would most likely be to tell her this store, like all the others, was closing.

Madison forced the thought from her mind, afraid the other woman would see it on her face, and let the manager give her an official, and useless, tour of the store.

Madison nodded and smiled, and silently ground her teeth, until she could make the excuse of needing to get back to the office and escape.

Once in her car, she didn't even stop to do the sketches before she drove away.

Why bother? Without Jake's help, Dartmoor was doomed. If only she'd paid more attention to what was going on these last few years. Her grandfather had left her ten percent of the company, but made her father trustee until she was twenty-two. Since her father had stopped speaking to her after she'd left Jake at the altar, to insist on voting her shares once she technically could would have been more of an emotional minefield than she'd been willing to risk.

She'd hoped that once she had her MBA, her father would do more than let her vote her own shares – he'd train her to take over Dartmoor someday.

She blinked away tears. That would never happen now. His death had robbed her of the future she'd wanted and left her nothing but anger with him over the past.

As traffic slowed to cross the bridge, a dark new suspicion appeared to rearrange that past to form a picture she'd never considered before.

Maybe the money he'd wasted on her wedding wasn't the real reason her father had shut her out of his life. If she'd been on speaking terms with him and asked too many questions about Dartmoor, she might have discovered the truth about the new CFO he'd hired. In fact, if she hadn't been such a coward and had insisted on voting her shares, she might have been able to stop this whole disaster before it started.

She pulled off the freeway, wound through the traffic to the garage under the apartment building, and punched in the code. The metal doors ground open.

She'd pay for her cowardice now by having to tell her mother they had only one choice left – close down the business their family had owned for over a hundred and fifty years.

Madison parked the car and rested her forehead on the steering wheel. The garage door ground shut behind her like a prison gate. What she needed was a miracle.

Chapter Three

Madison worked to conceal her nervousness, and her grief, as the salesman inspected her beloved Ferrari in the mildly noxious air of the "previously owned" imported car lot.

Two days after her dinner with Jake, she'd accepted that she was out of other options. At least for now.

Once the salesman had checked under the hood and gone over the pristine red paint job, he slid into the driver's seat and turned the key. The engine roared to life, then purred contentedly, forcing Madison to step away from smell of the exhaust. He pushed in the clutch and ran the shifter through the gears before he left it in neutral, climbed out and stood a moment watching the fine gray smoke that came out its tailpipe. Then he walked back around and reached inside to turn off the key, which he handed to her with a little shake of his head.

She could see the little "no" sign in his right eye and "sale" in his left, like an old cartoon.

"It's in great shape for a vintage car." He ran a beefy hand through his hair. "Wish I could take it off your hands, but who knows how long it would sit on the lot before someone showed up who could afford to buy it. I can't tie up that kind of money in slow-moving inventory."

"What if I offered five percent above the usual commission?"

The man leaned back against the fender of the dark-blue Bentley parked next to her car and stared at his shoes, obviously doing a few quick calculations in his head.

"Nope. I could take it on consignment for you."

"I'm afraid that won't work."

Madison needed the money now. Her trust fund was running low. An infusion of cash from selling the Ferrari, as much as it would break her heart, would stretch her inheritance out a few months longer. Maybe long enough for her to find new financing for Dartmoor.

"Can you refer me to other imported car dealers in the area who might be interested in buying it?"

The man shook his head. "Don't think there's anyone who can do more than I can, but I'll email you a list." He took her business card. "I'm sorry. It's a great little vehicle."

She nodded, climbed into the car, and backed carefully out of the lot while her mind sorted through what few options she had left. She quickly discarded the idea of putting the car up for sale on the internet. She'd never get the kind of money it was really worth.

She refused to admit to a flicker of relief that she could keep the car she loved after all.

Jake stretched, then linked his fingers behind his head. Across the conference table his personal assistant typed data into a spread-sheet, her shiny black hair bouncing slightly as she nodded over the numbers.

For maybe the hundredth time in the two years she'd worked for him, he wondered why he liked Astrid so much, enjoyed her company so much, found her attractive and yet felt zero, less than zero, sexual attraction for her.

And she'd made it clear she had the same reaction to him.

The exact opposite of Madison. Even after all that had happened, he could barely think of her without wanting her. A reaction that had only gotten worse in the two days since their dinner at the

Yacht Club. She was like a drug – one he needed to resist or risk ending up like his father.

His cell buzzed. "Number unknown." He had nothing to do while Astrid ran the data, so he took the call.

Five minutes later he clicked the phone off and stared out window, absently drumming his fingers on the table.

"What?" Astrid looked up with a frown of annoyance.

"Nothing."

"If it was nothing, you wouldn't make that irritating noise so I'd need to ask about it."

He quieted his fingers. This wasn't something he could discuss with Astrid, but she was right. He needed to talk about it with someone. If only his father. . .

But relationships hadn't been his father's strong point, either.

He stood to pace across the room and stare at the portraits of his father and grandfather that hung on the wall by the door. But he wasn't seeing them. He was seeing Madison's face the day he handed her the keys to the Ferrari. The tears in her eyes hadn't been because of the car itself – it wasn't until later that she'd come to love it so much – but because he'd known her well enough to buy her exactly what she'd wanted most. Because he'd loved her that much.

Now she was trying to sell the car. The salesman who called hadn't realized it was the same car Jake had bought from his company four years ago, but had thought Jake might be interested in a matched set of the rare vintage cars for himself and his "wife." A distress sale, the man said, so Jake would get a good deal on it.

Which didn't resolve the question of whether Madison was selling the Ferrari to break the last tie between them, or was in more dire financial straits than he'd imagined.

He waited until he and Astrid had the numbers crunched, then picked up his phone, fingers shaking like an addict as he punched in Madison's cell number.

She hadn't changed it. The sound of her voice, the stress he heard in her "Hello," left him momentarily speechless.

He swallowed. "Hey."

"Who is this?"

"Me. Jake."

She drew in a sharp breath. "What do you want?"

He almost said, "A second chance." At what he wasn't sure.

"I was a jerk," was safer.

"There's a news bulletin."

He ignored the prick of irritation. "I shouldn't have said I'd look at your plan and then brush you off. I'd like to make it up to you."

He wasn't sure what response he'd expected, but not the hollow sound in her voice.

"What do you have in mind?"

Nothing, right at the moment.

"Can you come by the office this afternoon? I'll go over your plan and see if there's some way I can arrange a small bridge loan for you."

"Really?"

"I owe you."

"All on the up and up?"

He probably deserved that, but it still rankled.

"I said I owe you."

"Would three o'clock work?"

Once they'd set a time he cleared his calendar and did two or three hours of work in a little over an hour.

Which left him no time to wonder why he would even consider lending money to a failing business in an industry he knew nothing about.

Madison had dreaded a repeat of the walk down the corridor to Jake's office, but when she found him waiting for her by the elevators it only fed her suspicions about what new game he might be playing.

He made pleasant small-talk as they went through to his office, where he sat her at the large conference table and waited with a politely expectant smile, as if she were a total stranger.

He didn't seem to notice the way her hands shook as she opened the leather briefcase and took out her tablet computer. He listened to the presentation she'd so carefully prepared, then he shuffled through the printouts she'd brought to back up her cost estimates and income projections. She fought the urge to squirm while Jake read Dartmoor's latest audit.

That was the most recent financial data she'd been able to get without telling anyone at Dartmoor about her appointment with Jake. She still didn't want to build anyone's hopes up. Of course, things would be much worse now the ex-CFO had cashed in her golden parachute, but the auditor's report was bad enough.

After what felt like a very long time, Jake lifted his head and gave her a look she couldn't quite decipher.

"Your father really messed up, didn't he?"

She bridled, surprised at the impulse to defend the man who was responsible for this whole nasty situation.

"He didn't exercise proper oversight, no."

"Why'd he hire such an incompetent CFO in the first place?"

"She was supposedly brilliant at another chain."

Jake opened a file with the woman's beautiful, cold face. Madison turned her head away.

"It's a long step from financial analyst to CFO, but I'd guess her business skills weren't the real reason your father hired her."

"Let's refocus on my plan, shall we?"

"How successful your plan will be depends on what kind of resources Dartmoor has to carry it out."

She wondered what was going on behind the polite mask he'd worn ever since he greeted her, but the face she'd once been able to read like a book was closed to her.

"That's why I included the audit. It's out of date, but the numbers can give you a rough idea of our current financial situation."

31

"'Rough' describes your situation pretty well."

She swallowed a sharp retort. She'd expected him to be a little gentler in his comments. He'd called the meeting, after all. It was as if just being near her irritated him, the same way being near him made her nerves dance along the jagged edge between grief, anger, and desire.

He set the papers aside. "Remind me of how much money you want, exactly."

She took the tablet and shuffled through her slideshow to the screen with the final figures, then gave it back to him.

"With that I could do the most important updates at one of our stores. Once it's clear the updates can make it profitable again, we can obtain more financing from our usual sources to roll them out in our other locations."

"Your mother must have other assets she can sell to raise the capital you need."

Here it came. Madison squared her shoulders and shifted back in her chair.

"My father dug himself in deeper than you think. He'd been quietly selling mother's other assets over the last few years to balance the books at Dartmoor. Shortly before he died, he even sold the condo here in town and moved in with his mistress-slash-CFO."

Jake swore, quietly but colorfully. She didn't blame him.

"Your mother had no clue?"

"Mother left my dad right after. . .when he stopped speaking to me. She didn't have any say in what he did as long as she stayed married to him, in any case. Grandfather Moore left everything in a trust, with my father as trustee."

"Which would explain why your mother didn't divorce him."

"That, and the fact that she never stopped loving him."

Jake swore again. He knew enough about unhappy marriages from his own parents' to understand why Madison's eyes clouded over with a lifetime of little sorrows.

He scrolled through the presentation and pretended to go over the numbers again while he wondered what he'd gotten himself into and how to get himself out of it. In his eagerness to solve Madison's problem for her, he'd made two major miscalculations.

The first was that Dartmoor's financial situation was much worse than he'd expected. He saw no way to justify a direct loan for Dartmoor to the Board at Carlyle's. He'd be as bad as her father if he based it on nothing more than his feelings for Madison, whatever those feelings were. And he didn't have enough liquidity to raise the cash from his other holdings for a personal loan. He hated it that he couldn't help her.

His other big mistake was underestimating how strong his feelings for Madison still were. Their dinner together had been about closure, moving on with his life. He'd quickly learned what a stupid illusion that had been. He doubted now there was any way in the world to get this woman out of his system.

Even now his body hummed with wanting her, despite the opposite-of-sexy conversation, but the last hour had reminded him of all there was to how he felt about her besides sex. The delicate scent of her perfume calmed him at the same time it aroused him. He wished he was able to drink in the sound of her voice so he could hear it when she wasn't there. Her every move, the shape of her hands, her rare smiles intoxicated him.

Not to mention the psychic slap to the head he'd gotten once he realized how clever her plans for Dartmoor really were. She was damned good at what she did.

Absently he flipped through the screenshots. A stray fact he'd missed caught his eye.

"Why does my mother own ten percent of Dartmoor?"

Madison gave a rueful laugh. "My father talked your father into buying it while you and I were engaged. At one point my dad owned a small share in Carlyle & Sons, too. I guess your dad held on after we didn't. . ." She gestured vaguely with her ringless left hand.

Something clicked in Jake's brain. Madison's mother owned sixty percent of the company. Madison held another ten percent, as did his mother and two other shareholders.

The pieces fell into place – how he'd be able to help Madison. How he'd be able to have her back in his bed, in his life, which, he saw with stunning clarity, had been his goal all along.

How he'd be able to do it all, have it all, without letting her know how much her desertion had hurt him, or how badly she could hurt him again.

It was a gamble, a big one, but one he was willing to take.

"I'm sorry," he said, "but there isn't enough here to justify a loan from Carlyle's."

Instead of slumping back in defeat as he'd expected, she sat straighter and leaned toward him. "If you can loan me half the amount, I might be able to raise the rest from friends."

"No."

"A personal loan?"

He shook his head. "Not possible."

A momentary wave of grief crossed her face, but she quickly hid it. Methodically she closed her tablet and gathered her papers, then put them neatly into her briefcase. She looked at him one last time, as if to gauge whether to say more, but he kept his feelings carefully masked. She pushed her chair away from the table.

Timing, keeping her slightly off-balance, was vital. She was half out of the chair when he allowed his voice to soften and said, "Madi."

Madison sat down and lifted her chin. She didn't trust the expression on Jake's face.

"There might be a way."

Now she really didn't trust his expression. "How?"

"What if I bought two-thirds of your mother's shares in Dartmoor?"

He cited a number that made her tense her jaw to stop it from

34

dropping open.

"That should give you the capital to update two or three of the stores," he added.

"I thought you couldn't come up with that kind of money."

"Not as a loan. But as an investment it would be worth borrowing against some of my other holdings."

"But what if you lost it all!"

He looked as surprised as she was at her reaction, then gave her a slow grin.

"I'd still be, as you put it before, 'filthy rich.'"

She cringed at the reminder while her pulse raced. There might be a way to save Dartmoor after all!

But the expression on Jake's face still worried her. She ran through the numbers in her head and found the trap.

"Two-thirds of Mother's share is forty percent of Dartmoor. With your mother's share, you'd own fifty percent."

He chuckled. "That gives me a lot more control over what my mother does than I'm likely to have. Besides, you, your mother, and the other current shareholders will have fifty percent, too."

"Which might lead to a deadlocked board."

He leaned closer and put his hand over hers. She resisted the urge to pull away, but his touch sent a shockwave of need through her system that played havoc with her concentration.

"Let's not assume the worse. We can always put something into the legal papers that would allow you to buy part of my share if the Board should ever be deadlocked."

More was going on behind those bright-blue eyes. She was sure of it. If she could just think more clearly. She wiggled her hand slightly to free it from the mesmerizing effect of his touch. Slowly her head cleared enough to see the flaw in his plan, draining the glow from the possibilities in front of her.

"If we reinvest all the money you give us into Dartmoor, what will Mother live on?"

He released her hand and made a sweeping gesture. "You could

35

invest some of it elsewhere to provide her with a decent income. But that probably wouldn't leave enough to make the difference in Dartmoor's bottom line. You need to attract outside financing."

Dark suspicions swarmed into her mind. She could hear her grandfather say, "If it sounds too good to be true, it probably is."

"Ah, so there's a catch. What more do you want from us, besides the shares? You wouldn't do this simply to make up for dinner the other night. Or out of friendship."

"The 'catch,' as you put it, is that I want you to marry me."

"What? Are you crazy?"

He reacted more quickly than she did. The bland mask lifted for only a moment to reveal the flash of anger and hurt in his eyes before it fell back into place.

"That's not how you reacted the last time I asked you to marry me. If I remember, you were very pleased. You even cried. It was quite touching, actually. Fooled me completely."

Her head already in a spin, she grasped the arms of her chair to help anchor herself in some sort of reality.

"Fooled you?"

"I thought you loved me."

Her heart twisted. She closed her eyes against the bitterness of his words.

"I d–d-did love you."

He brushed the confession away. "And how long did that last?"

Hurt almost beyond bearing, she hid the wound behind the anger that was her only protection against this man.

"Until you tried to take over my life. Choosing between my dream of running Dartmoor someday and being your trophy wife wasn't much of a choice. Certainly not one a man would force on a woman he loved."

If some weak part of her hoped he'd respond to her charge as she responded to his, she was doomed to disappointment.

"We've had this conversation," he said instead. "You misinterpreted a chance remark and used that as an excuse to walk out on me."

Anger roared in her ears. She struggled to calm the pounding in her heart and the churning in her stomach.

"So that's what your little joke was all about. Well, you've had your laugh. Can we let it go now?"

She half-stood again, but he stopped her.

"Joke?"

She didn't sit down again this time. She wasn't staying.

"About us getting married."

"It wasn't a joke."

She still didn't sit. She fell into the chair, legs too wobbly to hold her. Was this a dream? A nightmare?

"Why?" she asked in a raw voice.

He leaned toward her again. This time she had no urge to pull away, the sexual tug of his nearness no longer a threat. Or was it?

"I like you, you like me. We used to be friends. And we were great together in bed. Why not get married? You're CEO of Dartmoor, so no one can accuse you of being a trophy wife."

"I don't see why this would be a better deal for you than simply buying Mother's shares."

He gave her the wicked grin she knew so well. "Did you hear the part about great sex?"

Her emotions did a U-turn so fast she felt dizzy. She pushed herself to her feet, hoping her quivering knees would hold her.

"I'm not for sale, Jake." She headed for the door.

"Whoa!"

She kept walking.

"Not what I meant at all. It's the whole package, Madi."

The nickname was what made her stop. Made her hope.

"Friends, good sex, and I can help your mother out without having to explain it to anyone as a business decision."

And maybe you could learn to love me again. Not a good way to think right now. She needed to focus on the facts here, not go chasing rainbows.

37

But Jake had the facts on his side, too. Once her inheritance ran out, she and her mother would be homeless, unless Madison left Dartmoor and took a job somewhere else. Even then, it would take her a few years to earn enough to support the kind of life her mother had always led.

And they'd have to close Dartmoor. After putting up with a philandering husband her whole marriage to keep the family business alive, her mother would lose everything.

And all the employees who'd made Dartmoor what it was would lose their jobs. Her grandfather's voice again, reminding her this was about more families than hers.

All she had to do to prevent everyone from being hurt was marry the man she loved. Except, if she did that, she'd have to put her heart on the line, risk the pain of a loveless marriage her mother had lived with for years.

Madison wasn't sure she could do it. She wasn't sure she had any other choice.

She turned to face Jake. His careful mask told her nothing, but his blue eyes pierced through the center of hers, into her heart.

She held her head high as she walked back to the chair and sat down. "Give me the details of what would go into the pre-nup."

An emotion she couldn't name flickered across his face and disappeared.

"The usual. What's mine stays mine and what's yours stays yours. A clause about spousal support in case of divorce."

She clenched her jaw against a stab of pain, if not surprise, at his lack of faith in her business savvy.

"I won't need spousal support. Not after Dartmoor starts turning a profit again."

"What if I'm the one who needs it?"

The grin he gave her felt like sunshine after months of San Francisco fog. Her heart opened to the light like a flower.

This was not only the man she loved, he was also a man she could trust. He was nothing like her father. Even if she had no other choice, marrying Jake felt right.

As if he felt the shift in the air between them, he took her hand in his. The warmth of his touch burned from her skin down to parts of her she'd half-forgotten existed.

"Just to make it official," he said, "will you marry me?"

She blinked hard to stop the unexpected threat of tears – half joy, half fear. He must never know how much she still loved him.

"Just to make it official, Yes."

The simmering sexual tension between Jake and Madison built while they sketched out a pre-nup and the contract for his purchase of her mother's shares. By the time all the basics were set and he'd emailed them to his attorney, Jake's body ached with wanting Madison.

The half-hot, half-shy glances she threw him when she didn't think he would notice were reason to believe she felt the same way. The trick would be getting her from here to there – 'there' being his bed.

He hadn't planned on asking her to marry him to accomplish that, but the idea had settled into his mind with a satisfying click, like the missing piece of a puzzle. He didn't want to think too much about why.

Luckily he'd timed their meeting perfectly. "How about dinner to celebrate?"

Her eyes widened. "The deal's not final."

He flinched, but she was right. He could still lose her. One wrong move and he was toast.

"We haven't talked to my mother," she pointed out, "and the shares aren't mine to sell."

"Do you really expect her to say no to the chance to save Dartmoor?"

And if she does, will you still want to marry me?

Madison frowned. "Losing control of the Board may be important to her. Her great-grandfather built Dartmoor up from nothing. She might not want to sell it out of the family."

"If we're married, I'll be part of the family." He didn't wait for her answer, but went to his desk to push the intercom. "Selma, were you able to get that dinner reservation I wanted?"

"Yup," came the receptionist's voice. "But Astrid told me not to let you leave until she's had a chance to talk to you."

He mumbled his thanks. Business was the last thing on his priority list right now, but if Astrid thought it was important, it was.

When his assistant strolled in through the connecting door between their offices, she and Madison both threw him questioning looks.

"Madison, this is my personal assistant, Astrid."

Astrid was wearing her usual jeans and t-shirt, which she insisted were the main reason she preferred being a PA to the higher-level, but more visible, positions she was qualified for.

Madison gave her a long look and raised her eyebrows in a decent, if unintended, imitation of his mother's reaction.

"Astrid, this is Madison Ellsworth. My fiancée."

"Ellsworth? Isn't she the one who. . ." A smile broke across Astrid's. "Oooh! I love a happy ending. Congratulations, boss." She turned to Madison. "You take good care of him, now." Her voice dropped to a whisper. "He tends to work too much."

Madison seemed unsettled by Astrid's casual intimacy. Given her father's many infidelities, it made sense, but the last thing he wanted was Madison unsettled.

"Which is why you make almost more in overtime than you do in base salary," he told Astrid briskly. "Could we please get on with whatever it is you came in here about?"

Astrid immediately reverted to being the perfect PA. Within five minutes she had the input she needed from him and went back to her office, leaving an awkward silence in her wake.

"She's very attractive," Madison said.

"Yes, she is." He crossed the room and took her chin in his hand to turn her head so their gazes locked. "But you're the woman I asked to marry me."

40

The scent of Madison's perfume, the feel of her skin under his fingers worked the same magic they always did. Without allowing himself a chance to think, or Madison a chance to stop him, he kissed her.

Chapter Four

Jake's kiss erased everything from Madison's mind but an exquisite sense of coming home. She lifted her hands to hold his face as tenderly as he held hers and let the oblivion of her need for him wash over her like a healing spring.

When he finally lifted his head, she couldn't resist running her tongue along the tingle he'd left on her lips.

He made a sound that might have been a growl and stuffed his fists into his pockets.

"Did you drive here?"

"I took the cable car."

She'd learned to compensate for the necessary economy of a monthly Muni pass by using the cable cars whenever she could, even if it meant a longer walk.

"Good." He glanced down at his computer, probably checking his calendar for tomorrow. "Why don't we go now? We can have a drink before we eat."

"Where are we going?"

He winked at her. "That's a surprise."

She wasn't quite steady on her feet as he walked her to his black Lamborghini in the parking garage. Too many emotions jostled around in her brain, too many hopes, too many fears. She'd never dealt well with uncertainty, and she'd never been more uncertain in her life.

When he pulled the car up to a valet stand a few minutes later, Madison laughed.

"Top of the Mark? I don't think I've been here before."

"Didn't we come here for dinner on your prom night?"

"No, you were at Stanford then and took me some place down in Palo Alto. Who did you bring here on your prom night?"

The "oops" look on his face sent a chill down her spine, but he recovered quickly.

"It doesn't matter." He kissed her lightly. "I'm here with you now."

Despite her best efforts to keep her guard up, the night was perfect, the evening she'd dreamed of since she'd first fallen in love with Jake. They drank champagne, ate a gourmet dinner, and talked like the old friends they were. After dinner, they danced to a band of elderly gentlemen, who clearly loved the old-fashioned music they played. She doubted Jake enjoyed it as much as she did, but he smiled and nuzzled her ears as if he had nothing he'd rather be doing.

Which was lie. By the end of the evening, they both knew what they'd rather be doing. The only question was whether he would ask. And what she would answer if he did.

She pushed the problem out of her mind and floated around the room in Jake's arms as if the world began and ended right there. Which, she reluctantly admitted, for her it did.

Another chill ran through her when the band finally stopped playing and she found herself back in the real world.

She'd let herself fall too far into the daydream. If this turned out to be some kind of nasty revenge, she wouldn't land on her feet as easily as she had after the dinner at the Yacht Club. She'd be sucked back into the blackness that had almost defeated her after she'd walked away from Jake the last time. But she'd survived it once. She could again.

And for now Jake was making all the right moves, so she let herself relax.

Only when they were waiting for the valet to bring his car, huddled together for warmth in a world reduced by the fog to shades of gray and white, did he mention their next step.

"Come to my place for a night cap?" He nipped her ear playfully.

The nip, and the images that flowed from it like warm honey, made her say "Yes" before the more rational part of her mind had a chance to react.

"I'll take you home whenever you ask. I don't want to rush you."

"Why don't we play it by ear?"

He chuckled at her unintended pun and nipped her lobe again just as the valet appeared with the car.

Jake drove the short distance to the same building on the Embarcadero where he'd lived when they were engaged. But instead of his bachelor condo on the plaza level, a private elevator whisked them to the penthouse.

"I have to do a lot of entertaining for Carlyle's now," he explained when she stood drinking in the gorgeously decorated open floor plan with a grand piano poised in one corner. "Mother's been a bit of a recluse since Father. . ."

No one else would have heard the half-second pause, but Madison did, although she wasn't sure what it meant.

"Died," he finished smoothly.

"It's lovely." She ran her hands lightly across the keys of the piano without touching them. "When do you find time to take lessons?"

"I don't. I bought it as a wedding gift for you," he replied casually, then froze, apparently as shocked as she was at what sounded almost like a confession.

Years of training in the social graces paid off. Despite the need to blink away tears at the thought that he'd given her a second perfect gift without her even knowing, she managed an empty smile.

"Thank you. Rather belatedly, I guess."

"You always enjoyed playing. You called it your refuge."

"It was. You know what my home life was like. I'm surprised you kept it, though."

"Do you have any idea how weak the market is for high-end pre-owned pianos?"

Strangely disappointed by his response, she managed a laugh. "After I went away to college, my dad started calling my piano in the living room at home a ten-thousand-dollar paperweight."

"I'd never thought of it that way."

They stared at each other in the light from the entry hall. The fog stopped below the uncurtained windows in a surreal gray landscape of immaterial hills and valleys. The tops of brightly lit skyscrapers broke through the colorless blanket-like garish monuments to some alien god. Champagne still bubbled through Madison's system, but wariness and the memory of pain made her shiver.

"You should have worn a coat." He gestured for her to take a seat on the black leather sofa and gave her a down-soft cashmere throw he pulled from a clear acrylic cube that also served as a footstool. She wrapped the throw around her, as calmed by the gesture as by the warmth it provided.

"I didn't expect to be out so late."

"Will your mother be worried?"

She shifted her gaze to the glorious view. "She's visiting a friend in Carmel this week."

"How nice. For her, I mean."

Madison wasn't sure it was nice at all. Between the champagne and the effect of that smile, her willpower could have used some maternal back-up.

He slid off his jacket, loosened his ties, and touched a switch on the wall next to the fireplace, which roared into artificial life.

"Would you like something to drink?"

"The champagne. . ."

"You're not driving." He walked to the liquor cabinet hidden in one of the walls and lifted out a bottle. "Do you still drink Cointreau?"

"It's been a long time." Expensive liqueur didn't exactly fit into her current budget.

He must have taken her sigh for a yes, because he poured some of the amber liqueur into a small snifter and opened another bottle to pour two fingers of Irish whiskey for himself. He handed her the snifter, then pulled out a table from beside the leather chair across from the sofa. The top of the black acrylic box was inlaid with a familiar pattern of black and white triangles.

"Backgammon? At midnight?"

He took the black and white blots from a drawer in the table, two cups bound in black leather, and two pairs of dice. "Are you ready to go home?"

She shook her head, her face hot. He knew her well enough to guess she wasn't ready to go to bed with him yet, either.

She took a sip of the Cointreau and let the sweet orange liqueur burn down her throat while he pulled a black leather side chair over and sat opposite her.

He'd taught her to play backgammon, and for a while he'd been much better at it. By the time they got engaged, however, she'd been winning her share of games – not half but a solid third. She hadn't played since the wedding that never happened.

Tonight she won the first game easily. The second was closer, but at a critical point she slid her shoes off and stretched her legs to reveal the tops of the silk thigh-high hose she'd worn to his office to boost her confidence. Distracted, he misplayed and she took advantage of the error to win that game, too.

She assumed they'd stop there, but she hadn't counted on his competitive nature.

"Give me a chance for revenge?"

She ignored the threat that might be hidden in his question. "Sure, if you think you can beat me."

"I could use your strategy and take my shirt off, but that would be cheating."

"Are you calling me a cheater?"

He gave her another wolfish smile. "If the stocking fits. . ."

In the next game, when she stopped to take the last sip of her drink while she contemplated a particularly tricky move, he leaned back and unbuttoned his shirt.

"I thought that was cheating."

"What's good for the gander is good for a goose."

She started to correct him before she realized he was making a bad pun and laughed.

She won the third game by an even wider margin, leaving one of his men on the bar.

"Backgammon," she crowed, arms raised in celebration.

For a moment she thought he might be angry, but instead he grinned at her, slipped off the chair, and pushed the small end table to one side.

"Loser pays a forfeit," he said.

She ignored the flashing red alarm in the rational part of her mind and didn't offer any protest when he tugged up her skirt and moved her legs until he knelt between them. He looked up at her, his eyes hot. Intoxicated more by the man than the champagne and liqueur she'd had, she ruthlessly shut the alarm off and gave a small nod of acquiescence.

His grin became a sexy smile as he began to massage one of her ankles with each hand, his sensuous touch sending little bursts of desire up to her core. When she couldn't suppress a moan, he shifted to the backs of her calves, kneading the stress-tightened muscles until they melted under his touch. She fell back against the sleek leather of the sofa, all too aware of the hot dampness between her legs as her core melted, too.

He wasn't in any hurry. He found an unexpected erogenous zone behind her knees and stroked the flesh there until her head lolled against the cushions.

He didn't massage her thighs, but stroked them from knee to hip and back – first the top, then the outside, then the tender inside flesh. When he stopped at the top of each tantalizing stroke, his thumbs almost touched the thin layer of silk that sheltered the center of her desire.

She wanted to cry out in frustration, but something inside her refused to let him know how hot his erotic teasing made her. Instead she grasped at the unyielding leather and waited.

Finally, he slid his fingers between silk and skin to caress the vulnerable flesh hidden behind her panties. When she broke down and writhed erotically, he chuckled softly, pulled the panties off in a single gesture, and opened her legs wider, then lowered his head to send her to the stars with his tongue.

When she sank slowly back to reality, Jake was tugging her clothes back into some kind of order. That done, he sat beside her, lifted her hand to his lips, and kissed it.

"How many of your neighbors will notice if you don't come home 'til morning?"

She rolled her eyes at the idea of the dozen or so older ladies in the building who loved to gossip in the halls. "Too many."

"I think I need to take you home."

She sat up in surprise. "But I. . . You. . ."

"I'm a big boy. I can deal with it." He kissed her hand again. "What I can't deal with is the possibility you might spend the night in my bed and regret it tomorrow."

"I won't regret it," she told him, praying it was true.

"Well, maybe I would."

"What do you mean?" She swallowed to ease the crack in her voice. "Are you sorry you asked me to marry you?"

"No." He dropped her hand and leaned forward, elbows on his knees, and stared into the fireplace. "The opposite, in fact. It's just hit me what getting married means, or should mean. It's the kind of long-term investment that sometimes requires sacrifices upfront. This is one of those times. I don't want you to think tonight was all about sex."

She couldn't allow herself to take his earnest tone too seriously. "It was for me."

He brushed off her weak attempt at humor. "That's not so. You still hadn't decided you were ready to go to bed with me when we got here. And I didn't give you a chance to make a conscious decision about what happened between us."

She began to tell him the truth – that it didn't matter because she loved him, but she remembered that in all they'd said to each other in the last few hours, he hadn't said he loved her.

A chill crept over her. She picked up the cashmere throw and wrapped it around her again, but it didn't help. The intoxication of champagne, and sex, had faded from her mind, leaving her back where she'd been three years ago. In love with a man who didn't love her. Yet she'd agreed to marry him. She shivered.

They sat in silence, not looking at each other. Rain pelted the windows.

"There's another problem," he finally said. "I leave tomorrow for a four-week business trip to Asia."

A good reminder of how important she was – or wasn't – in his life.

"We can still transfer your mother's share in Dartmoor to me as soon as she agrees to it," he explained. "That's why I wanted to work out the details today. We'll be able to smooth out any remaining hitches with the lawyers via email."

When she couldn't find any words for the muddle of thoughts in her head, he went on.

"A month will give our mothers a chance to plan the wedding, too. I'd rather get married in the judge's chambers tomorrow before I leave, but they'll insist on making a big deal out of it. Just don't let them get out of control."

She gave a small laugh "You're assuming I have a whole lot more control than I've ever had over what my mother does, much less yours."

"You'll manage." He stood and paced to the fireplace. "It won't be easy, two CEO's married to each other. Once the Dartmoor Board approves your plans for the update, you'll be pretty busy."

"I'll manage," she echoed.

What else could she say? What else could she do?

He glanced at the Rolex on his wrist. "It's getting late. I need to get you home."

And she needed to get away from here, from him, so she could think clearly about everything that had happened today. The man, she realized much too late, had played her like a well-tuned piano, from the dramatic timing when he'd asked her to marry her to the champagne-induced moment of weakness that left her panties lying on the backgammon board.

Her face flamed as she stood, a bit unsteadily, whisked the offending scrap of silk up into her hand, and asked, "Where's the bathroom?"

His brow creased at the business-like tone she faked.

"Down the hall, on your right." His tone had cooled, too.

Probably a good thing. She needed to remember this was a business arrangement, a way to save Dartmoor. A business arrangement with benefits, maybe, but far from a love match. On Jake's side, at least. And she still couldn't be sure it wasn't his way of getting revenge.

When the housekeeper showed Jake into the breakfast room of his family home the next morning, he was struck, not for the first time, by what a beautiful woman his mother was. The streaks of gray in her dark hair only added drama to a face that had changed as little since it graced the covers of all the major fashion magazines as had her slender, well-honed figure.

Two years after his father's death, she'd never shown any interest in dating, much less marrying again. Survivors of good marriages were more likely to remarry than survivors of troubled ones, he'd once read. Still, his mother deserved a happier second half of her life.

"Champagne," she exclaimed when she saw the bottle in his hand. "My favorite label, too. Maribel, please bring us two glasses." Her smile dimmed and her eyes narrowed. "Or should I ask why we're drinking champagne for breakfast before I agree to join in on the celebration?"

All of the witty ways to tell her he'd come up with in the car on the drive across the Golden Gate to Belvedere vanished from his mind. "I'm getting married."

Her wary expression didn't change. "And the bride?"

"Madison Ellsworth."

Her face softened. "Sit down and tell me about it."

He joined her at the breakfast table that looked out the windows to the fog swirling over the Bay below them.

"There's not much to tell. We, er, ran into each other recently and realized the spark was still there."

Her mother raised her eyebrows. Lying to her was never a good idea, so he'd stick as close to the truth as he could and still protect Madison's privacy – not to mention her mother's.

"The idea just popped out at first." That was true enough. "We talked about it and when I asked her, she eventually said 'Yes'."

The housekeeper appeared with a second plate of eggs Benedict and two champagne glasses. He avoided any further explanation by busying himself with the bottle. When he'd poured the wine, he lifted his glass for a toast, but his mother held hers in both hands on the table.

"I must say I'm relieved," she said.

"Because Madison and I are back together?"

"Because it's not the awful brunette from your office who doesn't know how to dress! What's her name?"

"Astrid? Why would I marry Astrid?"

His mother shook her head and lifted her champagne.

"To you and Madison, and your future happiness."

They clinked their glasses and sipped the wine.

"When's the wedding, darling? At least six months after her father's death would be the standard time."

Here came the tricky part. "We decided to have it as soon as I come back from Asia."

His mother's eyebrows jumped. "You're kidding."

"We didn't see any reason to put it off."

"Why don't you live together for a while, if you're so hot for each other? What will people think?"

"That we're madly in love and couldn't bear to wait. We're not children, Mother, and we did the whole big wedding thing once already."

Her eyebrows shot upward again. She'd probably need an extra dose of Botox after this conversation.

She stared out into the fog and took a sip of her champagne. "I should say I'm happy for you, shouldn't I? I am, but are you sure this time, Jake?"

He wished he was, but his mother was the last person to share his doubts with. Instead he nodded and was rewarded with a real, Botox-be-damned smile.

"Good. I can't wait to go shopping for the perfect dress."

Whatever Madison might have expected her mother to say when told her daughter and Jake Carlyle were getting married, a sad "Oh, dear" would probably not have been on the list.

Dana Moore Ellsworth set down her tea cup and turned her eyes to the bay window that faced over the San Francisco Marina. Her friend had insisted on having her chauffeur drive Dana back to San Francisco as soon as Madison called to say she had important news, but the hurried trip had left her mother looking older and wearier than a woman her age should.

"I should have been the one to talk to Jake," Dana said. "I was afraid something like this might happen if you went."

Unsure how much to make of her mother's claim to clairvoyance, Madison took a sip of her coffee before she replied. The bitter taste helped her focus. She leaned back in the armchair and closed her eyes a moment.

"You're in no shape to do anything that stressful. Remember what the doctor said." She lifted her head to meet her mother's gaze. "I expected you to be happy about our plans. You were always fond of Jake."

"He's a lovely man, but. . ." Her mother made a vague gesture.

"I love him. And he loves me."

If only she was as sure of that as she sounded.

"That wasn't enough for you to marry him three years ago," her mother pointed out.

It was Madison's turn to look out the window. Sunlight glinted off the Bay, but the white caps were so high that only a few brave sailboats were out on the water.

"I was determined to get my MBA and help Dad out at Dartmoor, but Jake was dead set against me going to business school. I didn't want our marriage to start out with a conflict that basic lurking under the surface."

Not the whole reason, but her mother would never understand how important it was to Madison to live her own life and never be dependent on a man, the way Dana had been on Madison's father. So dependent she'd had to tolerate his cheating and couldn't divorce him even when his infidelities became blatant enough to make the local gossip blogs. Three years ago Jake hadn't understood how important independence was to Madison, but now he did.

She hoped. Despite her earlier sense of rightness about the marriage, second thoughts had bounced around her mind since she'd gotten a text message from Astrid to tell her Jake was tied up in a meeting and wouldn't have time to call Madison before his plane left for Asia.

Once one doubt had reared its ugly head, a host of others had swarmed in after it. But there was no reason to worry her mother with all that.

"He expected you to be a full-time wife, like his mother," Dana said.

"A trophy wife, you mean? He knows better now."

At least she'd told him so. The question was whether he'd listened. She should have waited to tell her mother anything until

53

she'd talked to Jake again. Maybe he'd have said something to drive the doubts away. Or something to make her change her mind.

But she didn't have the luxury of waiting. They needed to move ahead on the transfer of the Dartmoor shares.

Her mother leaned forward and laid a hand on Madison's knee.

"You left him at the altar three years ago and he hasn't spoken to you again until this last week. I'd expect him to be after revenge, not marriage. It doesn't sound like the recipe for a happy life to me."

The word "revenge" forced Madison to her feet. She went to the Victorian whatnot in the corner of the over-filled apartment. The comforting scent of her Grandmother Moore's favorite lavender perfume clung to the wooden shelves covered with Nana's collection of small china dogs. Absently Madison picked up a sleeping dachshund.

"We've worked it out." Maybe not yet, but they would. When things settled down.

"All the same, I wish you weren't rushing into this."

Madison set down the dachshund and picked up the golden Pekinese she'd given Nana the Christmas before she died.

"I love Jake. I've dreamed of marrying him since I was twelve years old. How can that be a bad thing?"

"There's much more to marriage than loving someone." Her mother closed her eyes. "It's my fault you and Jake have to get married in such a rush."

Madison flew back to sit in the chair. "No, it's not. We all know whose fault it is, and it's not yours."

Her mother flinched and Madison rushed on.

"Besides, it's not a matter of fault."

Her mother shook her head. "I should have moved some of my assets into my name, no matter what your grandfather's will said. I assumed your father would always take care of us, so I didn't force the issue with him. I didn't want the hassle, as people used to say."

"It'll be okay. Please be happy for me."

"You be happy for you." Her mother stroked Madison's cheek

with a hand that wasn't quite steady. "That's more important."

"I—we will be happy." She hoped her mother didn't hear the doubt she couldn't erase from her voice – or her heart.

Chapter Five

Madison quickly decided that if the months before the wedding-that-never-happened had been a run-away train, the weeks before this one were a hurricane. Both her mother and Jake's became forces of nature. Wisely, Jake had assigned them each their own areas to supervise. Rachel Carlyle was in charge of wedding announcements and the luncheon. Dana Ellsworth was assigned the task of organizing the judge, the flowers, and her daughter, since everyone apparently considered the bride-to-be unable to do anything.

Which wasn't far from the truth. Acting as CEO of Dartmoor under the current conditions was a full-time job. The meetings, video conferences, and endless phone calls with her mother's lawyer and Jake's to work out the sale of her mother's shares took what scant time remained in Madison's day.

Luckily, her mother agreed to relinquish the shares with only a little persuasion. "If you're married to Jake, I suppose the business will still be in the family."

Madison wasn't happy about the extra pressure to make her marriage a success, but it would be worth it to have the money to save Dartmoor.

In between her job and working out the sale of the Dartmoor shares, she consulted with a friend of hers who practiced family law and another of Jake's lawyers to hone a pre-nuptial agreement they both could live with. In fact, more of the time she and Jake spent on the telephone or video-conferencing each day was about the pre-nup than the Dartmoor deal, but she finally convinced him to limit any spousal support to one year in the case of divorce.

If she didn't make Dartmoor profitable in a year, she insisted, she deserved to end up working in a cubicle somewhere in Silicon Valley.

He chuckled, then growled, "What color panties are you wearing?"

Telephone or video sex – all talk in either case – had become a regular part of their conversations. The words made her uncomfortable at first, but when he'd sensed her hesitation and backed off, she missed the erotic intimacy. The first time she asked him what color briefs he was wearing, he'd burst out laughing.

"I love. . ."

She couldn't tell whether the shadow that passed over his face was a glitch in the internet connection or not.

"I love it when you talk dirty," he finished.

She'd managed to give a throaty laugh, but the words he didn't say dredged up old fears.

Yet, as the day drew nearer and the legalities were resolved, she managed to ignore her doubts and slipped into the same floating, dream-like state she remembered from the first time she was supposed to marry Jake.

One afternoon, when she returned to Dartmoor headquarters after a visit to the Walnut Creek store, a small square box lay waiting for her on her desk. She opened it to find the diamond, emerald, and sapphire ring she and Jake had designed for her when they were engaged the first time. She allowed herself a sentimental cry, and from then on sleepwalked through the preparations, never quite coming into contact with reality.

Toward the end it was almost as if she and her mother had reversed personalities. Dana made endless lists, bullied their hair stylist into opening his salon at seven a.m., and ruthlessly vetoed Madison's plan to wear a dress she already owned, a dove-gray silk she considered perfect for the occasion.

"His mother will be scandalized if you don't buy a new dress," Dana said in dismay.

"She won't know it's not new."

"And gray! No, dear."

Madison shook off the semi-dream state she'd been in long enough to take a stand. "I will not wear white."

Her mother gave her a look.

"Not so soon after Father's death," Madison explained in a rush.

"Of course not. Ivory or cream would be nice, don't you think, dear?"

What Madison thought obviously didn't make much difference, but her one moment of clarity passed and she sank back into the now-familiar haze of hope and suppressed dread.

By the time she stood in front of the mirror in her bedroom in the cream silk suit her mother deemed appropriate and watched in the mirror while Dana arranged the cream-colored hat with the tiny white veil just so on Madison's elaborate up-do, she might as well as have been sleepwalking. When Jake's limo arrived, she floated rather than walked to the elevator.

Later she didn't remember arriving at the San Francisco's Beaux-Arts City Hall or the trip up to the judge's chambers. Only when Jake appeared at her side and handed her a bouquet of gardenias – the same flowers he'd bought her on their first date – did the world snap into focus.

His flight home had been delayed and he'd gotten in very late the night before. At the sight of him, picture-perfect in a light-gray suit with a cream-colored shirt and a plain blue tie that, by some magic of her mother's, matched her silk blouse, joy beamed through the haze. She was marrying the man she loved.

She listened to every word of the ceremony, swept up in the magic. Her "I do" was pure music, Jake's baritone "I do" the perfect harmony.

Her hands shook as he slid the ring on her finger, but stilled as she did the same with his plain gold band. When she turned to kiss him for the first time as his wife, she was certain he'd see in her eyes all the love and happiness dancing through her. She hoped to see the same in his, but he'd already half-closed his eyes as he bent his head toward hers.

As Jake lowered his head toward Madison's he realized this would be the first time they'd kissed in a month. The kind of kiss he wanted, burned to give her, wasn't appropriate in front of an audience, especially one composed of their mothers, an elderly judge, and a scattering of aunts, uncles, and cousins.

But Madison's expectant look overrode his hesitation.

God, she was beautiful. And happy. The weight of Dartmoor's financial problems must have been heavier than he thought, if solving them gave her such a glow.

He dipped his head and kissed her. The searing burst of raw lust the simple contact sent through his body made him gasp. Abruptly, he pulled away.

He didn't understand the anguished expression that crossed her face. When he took her hand, it quivered in his, but she stood solid beside him and gave a much lower-wattage smile to their assembled relatives.

In the limo on the way to the Yacht Club for the wedding lunch, he wanted to ask her what was wrong, but she didn't give him the chance. She chatted emptily about the ceremony and the people there, until he reached up to capture her chin between his fingers.

He didn't even know what to say. "Shut up" was all wrong. "I love you" was too risky. Stumped, he kissed her again.

This time she was the one who gasped, but she didn't pull away. Instead she put her arms around his neck and lured him deeper into the intoxicating heat of her mouth, the erotic scent of musk and flowers that was, had always been, Madison.

He reached up and touched not her soft, lovely hair, but the stiff little hat her mother must have chosen for her. He caressed her neck instead, delicate skin hot under his touch.

When he slid his tongue across the line of her lips, she opened for him, drew him in. His pulse raced and his hard body rebelled against the perfect fit of his tailored trousers.

Vaguely he remembered intending to talk to her, but now all he could think of was the aching need she inspired in him. He slid his free hand up the curve of her breasts and was on the verge of dipping inside the neckline of her blue silk blouse when the limo came to a halt. They both jumped back at the same moment.

The Yacht Club doorman standing by the car winked at him, then gave them time to recover before he opened the door with a flourish.

As red-faced as teenagers caught necking on *Twin Peaks*, they found the rest of wedding party waiting for them. When he shot his driver a quizzical look, the man shrugged.

"You seemed to be enjoying the ride, so I took the long way, sir."

At least the driver hadn't prolonged the trip more, or the doorman would have gotten a real eyeful.

Jake took Madison's hand – rock-steady now – and kissed her temple. "Later," he growled and she gave a gratifying laugh.

The pleasure her laughter gave him sent a new shock through him, and not a pleasant one.

He'd just given this woman, who'd already walked out on him once, the power to put him in a world of pain. His only hope was that she'd never know how much he needed her in his life.

Jake's relatives far outnumbered Madison's mother and her father's brother at the wedding luncheon, but her Uncle Tyler took his role as substitute father of the bride to heart. He toasted them with warm words and good wishes Jake doubted her father would have been able to muster, and heartily welcomed Jake into the family.

"I can't wait to see what a bright young man like you does with Dartmoor," he told Jake as the party began to break up.

"I beg your pardon?" Jake shot Madison a glance so sharp she looked away.

Tyler Ellsworth slapped him on the back. "I'm sure you'll find a way to turn the company around now you're Chairman of the Board."

"I remember love, honor, and cherish," Jake said in an icy tone. "But I don't remember anything in the wedding ceremony about Dartmoor Department Stores."

"Didn't Madison tell you? Or did I forget to tell her?" Tyler gave a nervous laugh at the scowl Jake didn't bother to hide. "Since my brother's, um, untimely death, trusteeship for Dana's shares passed to me. As majority shareholder, I also took over as Chairman. After you bought Dana's shares, I called a meeting and the Board agreed that, as new majority shareholder, you should take over as soon as you get back from the honeymoon. No head for business, myself. I'm an engineer."

Madison turned to make an escape, a bit wobbly on her ultra-high heels, but Jake reached out and took her arm to hold her in place.

"What an interesting surprise." He managed a false smile.

He and Tyler both turned to Madison, who turned a charming shade of guilty red.

Why hadn't she told him about this one of the many times they talked while he was gone? Instead, she'd filled the time with mind-blowing sex talk. A pretty clever strategy. He'd begun to think maybe he could trust her, but she'd gone behind his back and tricked him again.

Jake did not need a second company to run. He'd worked so hard for so long to save Carlyle & Sons from bankruptcy after his father's death thrust him into the role of President. Now, when they were finally well into the black and he was able to think about some new initiatives, Madison drops a chain of department stores,

61

of all things, in his lap. Carlyle's was a shipping company. He didn't know jack about how to run a chain of department stores.

Before he could confront his scheming new wife, however, his driver appeared.

"Are you ready to go, sir? It's almost two."

Jake swallowed a curse as his mother and Madison's both descended on them. He prepared himself for the obligatory air kisses and what he always thought of as air hugs –– arms only, bodies not touching so as not to crumple the women's expensive dresses.

To his surprise, his mother wrapped her arms tight around him and squeezed. Hard.

Madison's mother held her daughter in a similar bear hug, which Madison was returning with interest.

"Good luck," her mother whispered.

He hugged her back, more gently, and kissed her cheek.

"Be happy, darling," she said.

"I'll do my best." The question was, was his best enough to keep Madison in his life?

And, after what he'd just learned, did he still want her there?

Madison sat tensely in the limo, her face still hot with embarrassment at her uncle's presumption that Jake would want to be chair of the Dartmoor Board. Why hadn't she been consulted? She knew the answer – because Tyler, while a sweet man, was her father's brother.

Not sure what to expect when she and Jake were alone again, she stopped herself just in time from wiping her damp hands on the skirt of her silk suit. That would leave a mark. Instead she set her bouquet on the seat and opened the tiny beaded purse that had been her grandmother's to pull out an Irish linen handkerchief with her mother's DME monogram in blue.

"The bride isn't supposed to cry," Jake said sharply as he climbed in beside her.

"Why would I be crying?"

"Maybe because you had to go through with it this time."

She stuffed the handkerchief back into the purse. "I told you why I never showed up at the church. . ."

"You did a lot more than not show up. You chose to walk out of my life."

"No. You shut me out of yours. I tried to contact you, Jake. You refused to answer my phone calls, return my emails, or respond to my texts. I did everything but go to your condo and bang on the damned door. I deserved a chance to explain, but you never gave me one."

His face was as impassive and handsome as the statue of a Greek god. "So explain."

"I already did. I didn't want to marry you then for a reason. It might not be a reason you accept, but it wasn't a whim, and I certainly didn't plan it ahead of time."

The limo picked up speed on the approach to the Bay Bridge.

"Speaking of planning things ahead of time," he said, "when did you intend to drop the little bomb about Dartmoor? In bed tonight?"

"I didn't know about it." She wound the handkerchief in and out between her fingers. "When Uncle Tyler told me about that last Board meeting, I didn't have the time to go, so I gave him my proxy. I didn't have any idea what he was up to."

"How convenient."

Anger prickled along her spine.

"If you won't believe any of my explanations about why I do what I do, this won't be much of a marriage."

"How much of a marriage it is remains to be seen."

Cut more deeply than she could have expected, she turned away. Sniping with Jake was bad enough. She wasn't prepared to be part of a marriage where they tried to hurt each other.

To hide the dampness of her eyes, she stared out at the pulse of the tides in the gray water underneath the bridge.

63

"Why don't you and your mother sell the damned department stores?" Jake asked in a milder tone. "You'd get plenty of cash from the deal for her to live the way she always has for the rest of her life."

"Could you sell Carlyle's?"

Now it was his turn to stare out at the water.

Finally he said, "Look, I don't know anything about department stores."

"You have to know more than Uncle Tyler does. You're President of Carlyle's. You know how to run a company, how to make money. If you don't know much about the industry, you hire good people who do. Our current COO and his management team are rock solid. All you need to do is hold a meeting once a quarter and Dartmoor will go on the same as it did when my father was Chair of the Board."

Except, of course, her father had been CEO, too. She'd be Jake's CEO. But fortunately that jagged little piece of reality hadn't worked its way into his jet-lagged consciousness yet.

"I guess your MBA wasn't a waste of time, after all. Any other gems of management wisdom to share?"

His sarcasm sucked the breath out of her lungs. She pulled her hand free and stared out the window again. They'd left the Bay Bridge and turned south onto the MacArthur Freeway.

"Where are we going?" she asked.

"It's a surprise."

The irony hit hard. "Oh, yes. We're on our honeymoon."

A honeymoon she'd been aching for and dreading by turns ever since she'd agreed to become his wife. What would sex with Jake be like, after so long? Her stomach did a little back-flip when she remembered the night at his penthouse.

At least the reminder seemed to have eased Jake's anger. He clicked on the satellite radio. The wail of a saxophone melted through the air. He hesitated, then punched a button. The swirl of strings in a Vivaldi concerto swept in to replace the mellow jazz he preferred.

Jake slid open a panel to reveal an ice bucket with a split of champagne. He opened the bottle and took two glasses from another hidden cupboard. The Waterford crystal glass he filled and handed to her was engraved with her name and the date.

"A gift from my Aunt Janice." He held up a matching glass engraved with his name.

"How sweet of her. I'll have to write her. Darn! I forgot about the thank-you notes."

"We'll be home tomorrow evening. You can write them then. There won't be many."

She remembered the endless notes she'd written to accompany all the gifts etiquette required she return after their wedding didn't happen. The memory threatened to darken her mood again, but she resolutely focused on the music and wine instead.

She'd had two – or was it three? – glasses of champagne at lunch, so this one left her head slightly muzzy. She must have dozed because when the limo rolled to a stop, she came back to full consciousness with a jolt.

They were parked on the tarmac of a small airport next to a private jet blazoned with the Carlyle & Sons logo. Since they were both so busy and they'd only be away for one night, she'd assumed they wouldn't be going far enough to fly.

As she followed Jake up the steps to the plane she asked him again where they were headed.

"It's a surprise."

This time he said it with a smile that sent a shock of need through her body. Worries aside, three years of celibacy was way too long.

"I love surprises."

He laughed. Maybe this marriage had a chance, after all.

Jake had more champagne stashed on the plane, but he'd forgotten what a light-weight Madison was. Three glasses of the bubbly had almost knocked her out for the count. He wanted her fully awake for the very private celebration he'd planned for her.

The plane circled out over the ocean before heading east, so it was a while before she figured out where they were going.

"Tahoe," she murmured once she did.

Her wonder, and the thinking he'd done while she dozed, made it easier to forgive her. Maybe she didn't know what the Dartmoor Board had done. Even if she did, she was right. He could pass off most of the work to the staff. He'd worked twenty-hour days when he'd taken over at Carlyle's. Being chair of the Dartmoor board couldn't add enough to his workload to top that.

And soon he'd have the wedding night Madison owed him – on his terms. When he took her hand in his, the electric charge sizzled through his nerves.

He'd flown to Lake Tahoe dozens of times since his father bought the plane, but Madison's family had always driven back and forth, so she'd never flown there. She was entranced by the vistas spread below them, despite her nervousness about small planes.

Or maybe her case of nerves was about him. For some reason, the thought pleased him. The more uncertain she was, the more of an advantage he had.

The perfect weather gave them an excellent view of the Great Valley. After the flash of gold atop the state capitol as they flew over Sacramento, the plane headed toward the rolling foothills of the Sierra Nevada.

He let her enjoy the trip in silence while he tried to control the erotic fantasies that crowded his mind – and the physical response that followed – but without much luck.

They were in the BMW convertible he kept at Tahoe and almost to his family's place before Madison realized why he'd brought her here.

"Jake." Her face lit up. "You darling."

He allowed himself a smug smile. Spending their wedding night where they'd first made love was one of his better ideas, given he couldn't afford to be away more than one night.

One night was all he needed. Once Madison was reminded of how good it was between them, leaving him would be the last thing on her mind. He hoped.

After they passed the turn-off for the big summer house her great-grandfather had built, and her father had been forced to sell, Madison remembered every step of the way to the Carlyle's house farther down the shore. After all the nights she'd snuck over there after her mother was asleep, she could probably have made the half-mile trip blindfolded.

She smiled at the memory of her first time alone there with Jake. They'd argued earlier in the day. They'd argued almost constantly that summer, in fact, the mounting sexual tension between twenty-two-year-old Jake and her barely eighteen-year-old self a constant source of unspoken conflict.

Where she'd found the courage to make the hike and knock on his door, well aware his parents were at the same party hers were, she'd never know. All she knew then was she needed to settle whatever it was they'd fought about that day before she went to bed.

He'd answered the door in the loose swim trunks he wore when he sailed, and she was lost. She wasn't sure either of them had spoken. She went into his arms, he kissed her, and the rest was a blur of joy, momentary pain, and incredible closeness. The ecstasy didn't come until later, but she'd been certain as soon as he'd opened the door he was the only man she wanted to share that sacred magic with her.

Jake parked in front of the familiar modern wood and glass A-frame, and asked her to wait in the car while he disappeared inside with their bags.

Her mind sank into memories of other nights spent here, some hushed and hurried so they didn't wake his parents, others slow and relaxed when he had the place to himself for a few hours. Always followed by the romantic walk together through the rich pine scent of the forest to her family's house. By the time she left for college, she'd been certain they'd always be together.

So much for the wisdom of an eighteen-year-old caught up in her first romance.

Jake, who must have forgiven her or, more likely, forgotten his earlier anger about Dartmoor, returned to open the car door and kissed her, just enough to stir her blood.

"Welcome back."

The gardenia bouquet she held in her hand filled the air with an erotic perfume as she stepped from the car, only to be swept up in Jake's arms.

"You can't," she laughed as he turned toward the open door of the house.

"I can try." He shifted her weight and she wrapped her arms around his neck. The bouquet bounced above his ear as he carried her, nodding its approval of the feat.

He slid her slowly down his body once they stepped inside the two-story great room. Beyond the sliding glass doors that flanked each side of the huge stone fireplace, beyond the deck, Lake Tahoe sparkled in the sunlight. The snow-capped Sierras added magic to the view.

She let herself lean against the strength of his shoulder for a moment, nearly as tall as he was in her high-heeled sandals. He kissed her cheek and led her down a hall to the master suite, where he took her bouquet and set it in a waiting vase.

Madison had never been in this room before. The king-sized bed faced out over the lake, but what caught her attention was one whole wall of sliding closet doors covered with mirrors. She couldn't imagine what it would be like to be able to see the two of them together in bed. The mirrors would reveal every intimacy.

That one little worry opened the door to a whole rush of others. To still the tiny swirl of mounting panic, she raised herself the inch or so necessary and kissed him.

Chapter Six

With a groan Jake took possession of Madison's mouth. She first retreated, luring him deeper in, then returned his invasion, as she rediscovered how to make him moan, how to make him clutch her more closely against the growing hardness of his body.

He was pondering whether to tumble her onto the floor or back her up against the wall before he realized they'd moved too far, too fast. He didn't want his raging hormones to turn their honeymoon into a triple-X-rated movie. At least not at first.

Slowly he pulled away. Her eyes were still closed, her mouth so lush and perfect he had to draw her near again, one arm tight around her waist. He raised the other to her beautiful pale-blonde hair where it rubbed against the stiff straw of the hat she'd worn for the wedding.

"Damn."

She laughed softly.

"How do I get this thing off?"

She stepped out of his embrace and lifted her arms. Two tiny movements and the pale straw shell was on the dresser.

She moved closer again, obviously eager to pick up where they left off, but now he was thinking more clearly he realized the frozen swirl of hair that was so lovely to look at would be a definite problem when it came to touching.

"Sit down."

She settled on the bench at the foot of the bed. He took off his jacket, turned her so he could sit behind her and pulled out all the hardware holding her hair in bondage.

"I can do it," she offered, but he ignored her.

When the last pin was gone, he ran his hand through the blonde flow he'd loosened, but it still resisted his caress.

"What can I do about this sticky stuff?"

"It needs brushing out. I. . ."

"Stay there. Brush in your overnight bag?"

She nodded, but her face flushed a sexy shade of pink.

He opened the bag and saw why. A shimmering, sheer piece of black-and-silver lace lay right on top. He sucked in a long breath when he found the matching panties underneath it and forced himself to imagine jumping naked into the icy lake outside. Luckily he located her hair brush without unearthing anything else to shift his body into overdrive. He sat down behind her and began to coax the gel and knots out of her hair.

For the first time Madison understood why some of her mother's friends had affairs with their hair stylists. She shivered with anticipation at the innocent yet erotic rhythm of Jake stroking the brush though her hair with the same patience and care she remembered him paying to more private parts of her anatomy.

She closed her eyes and let sensation take over, until it felt as if each stroke of the brush reached not only the ends of her shoulder-length hair, but clear down to her hot, damp core.

She made a soft purring sound. He answered with a gentle chuckle, but kept on stroking until the brush moved freely through her hair. Goal accomplished, he ran his fingers through it as well, massaging her scalp in a way that nearly sent her over the edge.

If it had been three days, not three years, since they'd been together, she would have demanded he take her. Instead, a strange shyness swept over her.

He went to put the brush on the dark-oak dresser that matched the vast sleigh bed, then turned toward her, waiting.

Her face heated as she stood, undid the buttons on her jacket and took it off. Aware of him watching every move, she opened one of the mirrored closet doors to hang up the jacket and her skirt. Carefully she slid the door shut and stared at Jake's reflection.

"I forget. Have we had sex in a room with mirrors before?" he asked in a casual tone.

She flushed, as much at his heated look as at the question, and shook her head.

"A hangover from the seventies." He shrugged. "If you don't like it, we can have them taken out. We can redo the whole place. But we're stuck with them for tonight."

Tonight didn't worry her. The lights could be turned off at night. But now reflections off the lake dappled the ceiling, despite the gauzy curtains across the sliding glass doors, and filled the room with the glow of the setting sun.

He must have sensed the reason for her hesitation. "If you want to wait. . ."

She turned to him, smiled, and reached up to undo the top button on her blouse. "I don't." Her hands froze. "Do you?"

"No." Two steps and his fingers touched hers. "Here, let me."

Instead of letting her hands drop, she rested them on his hips. He sucked in a breath and fumbled the third button. She giggled and tightened her grip.

He ridded her of her blouse, bra, and half-slip, but left her panties and her stocking, held up with traditional blue garters, and the cream suede high-heeled sandals. When he stepped back, she couldn't avoid what the mirrors revealed – the image of a woman bared to her lover for sex. Fascinated, she watched his reflection as she wiggled out of the panties.

His eyes were hot and hungry. "Beautiful."

She felt more than beautiful. She felt sexy, powerful.

She started toward him, but he stopped her.

71

"Touch yourself," he said. "Touch yourself the way you did when we talked about sex while I was in Asia."

The blast of need his words sent through her made it impossible to do anything but shift her legs apart and do as he said.

He swore softly. "Does it feel good?"

"Oh, yes." She swallowed. "But not as good as when you touch me there. Not nearly as good as when you. . ."

He swore again and turned away, then slid out of his shoes, and tugged off his socks.

The spell broken, she settled on the edge of the bed to watch his reflection as he quickly undressed. The shift in perspective took her by surprise when he suddenly stood in front of her wearing nothing but black silk briefs that emphasized his arousal more than they concealed it.

"Should I leave these on for a while yet?"

She didn't answer, but reached out to pull the briefs down. He looked down at her and stepped out of them.

The movement brought a tantalizing part of his anatomy directly in front of her face. He froze when she stroked the solid length of flesh.

"May I?" she whispered.

"Please," he let out on a rough breath.

She kissed and licked until he moaned again, then slipped her lips over the sleek end. He held her head in his hands, bringing back all the silky bliss from when he'd brushed her hair. When she took him deeper, his fingers fisted in her hair, the slight tugs a new, expected sort of sensual awakening. She settled happily in to return the favor he'd done her after the backgammon game, but he pulled away.

"It's our wedding day," he gasped.

"We have all day and all night. . ."

"Which is why what you have in mind can wait."

He dropped to his knees and claimed her mouth in a kiss so passionate it left her dazed. When she sank back onto the bed, he

72

lay beside her and held her in his arms. He kissed her again, slowly, reverently, a revelation of sexual need and much, so much more.

She responded in kind, everything she felt for this man flowing into the almost unbearable heat that grew between them as tongues dueled and hands caressed, explored, enticed. The silk brocade of the bedspread under her body added an unexpected layer of sensual torment to the impatient gentleness of his touch. The rich aroma of the gardenias, blended with the musky scent of his body, lit tiny fires of desire all through her.

They were both too aroused for the erotic play to last long. When he entered her, her whole body seemed to take flight, soaring higher as he possessed her more fully. Instantly the glowing light he lit inside her exploded in a cascade of color and sound.

Her soft cries echoed with his deeper sounds of pleasure as he paused to allow the moment to fill them both. Her body floated, half sated, half burning with desire for more.

He began to move again, sending new waves of delight through her as he rushed them both headlong toward another, brighter moment of ecstasy, the light becoming crystal fire that consumed her, consumed them entirely.

Her shattered self came together bit by shining bit until she awoke to the butterfly touch of Jake's kisses on her face.

"Sorry," he said.

She raised a languid hand to his mouth. "Don't you dare say anything. It was perfect."

He grinned. "Yeah, it kind of was, wasn't it? Instead I'll tell you about how more perfect the next time will be. And the next, and the next."

She gave him a dreamy smile and let her eyes fall closed.

She already felt the stirrings in her body, and his, that signaled the next time wasn't far away. The need to confess how much she loved him before they danced the ancient dance again rolled through her with an almost physical ache.

But his silence said more than any words. She closed her eyes more tightly to shut out the emptiness.

The next night Jake sat at the desk in his home office back in San Francisco and stared at the numbers in front of him with growing disbelief.

The woman he'd left thoroughly pleasured and asleep in his bed minutes before, intending to wake her and make sweet love to her all over as soon as he'd recovered, had duped him again. He'd thought, hoped, the love he'd read in those lying green eyes was real this time.

What a fool he'd been.

He sucked in a deep breath, letting the sucker punch resonate through his system, then stalked to the bar and poured himself a double.

Whiskey softened the edge, but barely. He took his glass back to his laptop to reread the documents Madison's Uncle Tyler had emailed him while they were on the brief honeymoon Jake had managed to carve out of his busy life.

He gave a rueful laugh at the profuse apologies he'd given Madison about needing to follow up on the Asia trip right away. She'd taken it so well he'd decided to arrange a real honeymoon in Paris as soon as he could free up a week for it.

The numbers in front of him made it clear he wasn't going to have a free minute for a very long while. Dartmoor Department Stores was essentially bankrupt. The money he'd paid for Dana Ellsworth's shares would be nothing more than a molehill on the mountain of the company's debt. Debt that had grown exponentially since the audit report Madison had shown him.

He should have insisted on seeing the latest financials. He should have known better than to trust her. He should never have agreed to look at her plan to save Dartmoor. He should have taken back the damned Ferrari after she refused to marry him and gotten a restraining order.

No, he refused to let the anger take control.

He scanned the spread sheets one more time. He was no accountant, but something about the numbers niggled at him. He copied the pages that bothered him and shot them to the accounting firm he used for his taxes and other personal needs. Odds were slim there was really anything wrong, but who knew what their forensic auditor might dig up.

An unexpected shot of guilt, over pursuing a more in-depth audit when Madison had consciously chosen not to, drove him from his chair again.

He went into the living area and paced the length of the darkened space, oblivious to the wonderland of lights below him. He hesitated when he passed the bar the second time around, but another drink wouldn't help. He needed to get past the anger – and the hurt that she'd lied to him he'd prefer to believe wasn't there.

Absently he drew his hand along the top of the piano as he passed it. He needed to calm down, work through the problem rationally.

"Jake?"

Madison stood in the door to the hall, her white silk robe hanging open to reveal her nakedness beneath it.

"Aren't you coming to bed?" The quiver of vulnerability in her voice lit a tiny flame of hope inside him. What if she didn't know how bad things were at Dartmoor?

He couldn't think clearly seeing her lushly naked body, with her looking at him with those wide eyes. "I'm not sleepy." Anger had seen to that.

"Oh."

After their rather athletic bout of sex not twenty minutes before, he didn't blame her for being surprised. Or maybe his gruffness surprised her. It was hard to act lover-like after what he'd just learned.

"You go on back to bed."

She nodded and disappeared into the bedroom, shutting the door softly behind her.

What if she didn't know?

He threw himself on the sofa and glowered at the empty fireplace, trying not to remember the night they'd played backgammon by firelight. Trying not to remember the last two sex-drenched days.

She'd said she let her uncle vote her shares in Dartmoor, and hadn't been at the most recent Board meeting. Of course, it might have been part of the plot, more lies to lure him into a situation where Carlyle & Son was forced to dig Dartmoor out of the hole her father had dug.

But if she intended to do that all along, it made no sense for her to bother with the plan she'd shown him to save Dartmoor. It was a good plan. It might even have worked if things hadn't gone downhill so fast since the last audit.

He lay on the couch, his silk robe wrapped around him. It always came down to the same question – whether or not he could trust a woman who'd walked out on him once. Maybe he should give her the benefit of a doubt this time. Or give her enough rope to hang herself.

He was still reviewing his options when the whiskey and great sex overwhelmed him and he fell asleep.

Madison lay awake in bed for an hour, waiting for Jake. She needed another half hour to summon up the courage to ask what had happened to turn him from the perfect lover back into the same cold stranger whose office she'd walked into six weeks before.

When she finally tiptoed down the hall, he wasn't at his desk. His laptop was on stand-by. The empty glass next to it smelled of whiskey.

She took the glass into the kitchen to rinse it when she heard a familiar snore.

He was in the living area, sprawled halfway off the black leather sofa. She started to wake him, but he looked so peaceful, despite his awkward position, that she settled for wrestling his second leg onto the cushions and brought the duvet from the guest room to cover him.

She brushed the hair off his forehead, as if he were a child, put a soft throw pillow under his head, and laid a kiss on his cheek before she went smiling back to their bed.

Jake watched the shock, pain, and anger on his wife's face over breakfast the next morning and wished like hell he was someplace else. Anyplace else.

"You're going to do what?" Her voice broke.

"I'm going to call a meeting of the Dartmoor Board and recommend that they – that we shut down the stores and liquidate the company's assets, effective immediately."

"But why?"

"Because the business is on the verge of bankruptcy and an orderly closing is in the best interests of the employees and the investors, including you and your mother."

"Who are you to tell me, or my mother, what our best interests are?"

He raised one eyebrow. "Your husband?"

"You're my husband because I was trying to save my family's business."

There it was. He looked away to hide the mixture of triumph and grief she might see in his eyes. He'd given her enough rope to hang herself and she had. Dartmoor was still more important to her than he was.

He leaned forward on his elbows. "I can't rescue the company after years of your father's negligent, or just plain incompetent, leadership."

She flinched. He hated to hurt her, but at least his temper was under control. So far.

"My father may not have made a wise decision about this last CFO," she protested, "but he'd worked his way up at Dartmoor. I can't believe he was either negligent or incompetent."

"Your father married the boss's daughter and answered to no

77

one but himself and a Board composed of relatives and cronies. If the company had been publicly traded, the whole house of cards would have fallen down long before he hired a woman just so he could bang her."

She flinched again. Not his fault, Jake reminded himself with grim satisfaction.

"Do you have any idea how much the financial situation at Dartmoor has changed since the audit?" he asked her.

She chose to evade his question, not answer it. "Even if things are as bad as you say, you and I can get Dartmoor back in the black. You saved Carlyle's after your father let it fall apart."

Darkness swept across him. "My father was ill."

"I. . .I didn't know."

Later, when he wasn't feeling so vulnerable, he'd have to tell her the whole story about his father. Right now, she'd probably use the truth against him.

"Maybe the troubles at Carlyle's were for a different reason, but we can use what you learned to help save Dartmoor. With your experience and my plan, we can turn it around."

"Nice try, but I have one business to run. I don't have time to waste on a business that's already gone over the edge."

"You don't have to do it alone."

He shook his head. She might be CEO of Dartmoor, but even with her brand-new MBA, she'd never be able to clean up this mess without far more help than he had time to give.

"The only way I can see to keep Dartmoor from bankruptcy is a massive infusion of cash from Carlyle's," he told her. "My board of directors would never allow me to pour good money into a black hole. An orderly closing is the financially responsible option."

Her face had gone blank, shuttered. "How long do I have to talk you out of this?"

"As long as it takes me to arrange a meeting of the Board. But don't count on changing my mind. Facts are facts." He looked down at his breakfast and felt faintly sick. "Do you mind if I excuse myself and go on to work? I have a heavy day scheduled."

"No. Go ahead." Her determined expression told him this little game wasn't over yet.

But he'd win in the end. He always did. The real question was how much winning would cost him.

Madison finished her breakfast, then his, mind churning.

There must be a way to save Dartmoor. Her mother had lived in a dead marriage too many years to keep her family's business alive. Madison refused to let Jake shut it down.

She'd taken the week off work, so she spent the rest of the day in Jake's home office poring over the most recent financial documents. By afternoon she was forced to admit Jake was right. In fact, she didn't see how her father had kept Dartmoor running for the last couple of years.

The anger with her father that had tainted her grief since the day he died exploded into new levels of hurt and rage.

She closed the computer files in short, jerky movements. Then she went to the bedroom she shared with Jake, where she gave in to the need to rant and cry by turns until the tumult burned itself out and she slept.

When she woke up she was relieved to find a text message on her phone that Jake had a dinner meeting. Just as well. One look at her face right now would have revealed to him how deeply she'd been hurt by what she'd learned.

In the end, he didn't get home until she was asleep and left before she woke up.

She ate a lonely breakfast and drove the Ferrari across the Golden Gate after the first spate of rush-hour traffic. She was almost surprised to find the Dartmoor flagship store in San Rafael unchanged since she'd last been there, the night before her wedding. Somehow her imagination had morphed the familiar, solid building into a semi-ruin to match its financial state.

She lingered in the first-floor cosmetics department, stopping to chat with the sales staff and watching how the few early-morning customers moved through the traditionally configured space. What would it take to convince some of the biggest names in the cosmetics industry to let Dartmoor experiment with new ways to make their wares available and attractive to shoppers?

She took the escalator to the second floor and did the one-and-a-half circuits necessary to see how the day was going there and catch the escalator to the children's and men's departments on the third floor, where the sales staff outnumbered customers two to one. The same was true in the furniture and housewares departments on the fourth floor, but she did her best to be as cheerful in her conversations with the employees there as she had downstairs, where things were busier. Next she visited the hair salon tucked into one corner of the fourth floor, surprised to find more customers there than on the whole rest of the floor. Someone, probably one of the stylists, had chosen a soft country-rock station, and half the customers were singing along with Reba.

She rode the elevator to the offices on the upper floors, dim ideas forming in her mind.

In the foyer of the top floor she stopped, as she always did, to greet the unsmiling portraits of her father, grandfather, great-grandfather, and great-great-grandfather. "President and Chairman of the Board," they each said. She hoped she'd be able to keep Dartmoor afloat long enough for her portrait to hang there someday, too.

The administrative assistant did a double-take when Madison walked into the office suite she shared with Charlie Cochrane, the COO.

Her father's office, filled with the antique furniture of her great-grandfather's day, sat empty, a part of the past Dartmoor needed to move beyond.

"We didn't expect you back so soon, Ms. Ellsworth," the admin said. "We thought you were on your honeymoon." The woman grinned. "I guess it's Mrs. Carlyle now."

"Ms. Ellsworth is fine." She saw no reason to move two surnames away from the Moore family legacy. "Speaking of my wedding, I'll send you each a note later, but I want to thank you personally for the glass vase the staff up here gave us."

In fact, she'd been touched by all the gifts the people who worked for Dartmoor had sent, most bought with their employee discounts.

The admin smiled. "I'm glad you liked it."

"It's perfect for our mantel. You know how I love fresh-cut flowers, and I know who organizes the gift-buying around here. Thank you."

"You're welcome." The admin frowned. "Speaking of flowers, there aren't any in your office this morning. The flower shop didn't. . ."

"I told them not to."

Her week off had been as good a time as any to stop the twice-weekly delivery she'd indulged herself with when she first became CEO. Every penny counted.

She went through to her office and opened her files. Energized by the building full of people depending on her to save Dartmoor, she found a dozen ways to tweak her plan so it would work with the new financial information.

She went back to the penthouse early and set the revised presentation up on her laptop in Jake's home office, ready to show him why he didn't have to close Dartmoor after all.

She refused to consider what she might be forced to do if she failed to win him over.

Chapter Seven

Mrs. Lee, the housekeeper, must have sensed Madison had a some-thing special planned because she fixed Jake's favorite dinner, and gave Madison a grin before she left.

A few minutes later the penthouse's private elevator dinged. Madison's stomach tensed, but she was primed and prepared to do the sales job of her life. She got up from the piano, poured a glass of Jake's favorite whiskey and stepped into the entry as he came in the front door.

"Hello, darling." She smiled and held out the glass.

"No time for that, I'm afraid. Is dinner ready? I have tons of work to do."

She washed down the disappointment with a sip of the whiskey, grimacing at the fire that burned down her throat.

"I thought you were free this evening."

"I did, too, but I met today with the representative of a Japanese firm we've been trying to get as customer for years. I need to prepare for a video conference with the big boss. . ." He glanced at the clock on the wall of the entry hall. "In two hours. Prime time in Tokyo, sleepy time here."

"I was hoping to have a chance to talk to you."

He walked past her to put his briefcase in his office, pushing her laptop to one side without looking at it.

She followed him to the bedroom and took another sip of the whiskey.

"What's so important it can't wait until tomorrow?" he asked.

"I've updated my plan for Dartmoor, using the most recent financials."

He stopped in the middle of undoing his tie. "You really think you can make Dartmoor profitable? Do you have a plan to float the Titanic, too?"

She shrugged off the hurt. "Can't you spare a few minutes to listen to the changes I've made?"

"Not tonight. I'm sorry," he added, almost as an afterthought as he hung up his jacket and undid his cuffs. "Could you bring my dinner into the office? If I eat there, I might have a chance of sleeping tonight."

"Jake, we can save Dartmoor."

"And you and your MBA are going to show me how?"

His sarcasm was worse than she'd expected. She focused on her mother and the constant stream of infidelities she'd had to put up with instead.

"Dartmoor is perfectly positioned to move forward in the twenty-first century as the department store of choice for the suburban shopper who wants to juggle work, home and family, and still find time to take care of herself."

"Spare me the business-school-speak. Dartmoor is bleeding money. I need to get out of a sector I know nothing about and focus on Carlyle's core business."

Anger erupted inside her, propelling her ahead at full steam.

"Carlyle's core business is making money. You've moved into cruise lines, and now you're negotiating to buy a Caribbean resort. . ."

He walked past her to his office. "All natural outgrowths of the shipping industry, which Dartmoor is not. If your father hadn't left the finances in such a mess, I wouldn't have become chair of the Dartmoor Board in the first place." .

She didn't need to be reminded of why he'd married her.

"If you'd just look at my plan. . ."

"I've seen your plan. Adding a spa and direct access from in-store kiosks for home-delivery groceries will not save a department store chain that's lost money seven quarters in a row. Major money."

She shook off the undeniable truth and plunged on.

"It's more than the spa and the groceries. There's the redesign of the stores, new merchandise, new vendors. . ."

"All of which mean investing more money in a sinking ship."

"I've found some major cost savings and recalibrated the financing. I went over the numbers with Uncle Tyler and he's convinced we can turn Dartmoor around."

"Your uncle is only on the Dartmoor Board because he's your uncle. He's said himself he doesn't know how to sell women's clothes. Hell, even I don't know how to sell women's clothes."

Madison opened her eyes wide. She'd never considered the possibility that Jake might consider Dartmoor his failure. And he hated to fail at anything.

"Madison, it's not as if your mother will be penniless if we close Dartmoor."

The damned man knew her too well.

"The corporation still has considerable assets to liquidate, including six buildings in prime locations. She'll get enough money out of it to live the way she always has."

"This isn't about money. I'm not you. It's about what we can do with Dartmoor, how we can move it forward. Why kill my family's business, fire all those people, when we can save it?"

He ran an impatient hand through his already disheveled hair. "Because we can't save it. Closing it down is the only responsible thing to do. The Dartmoor Board meets next week. If I can't win over your Uncle Tyler, the other minority shareholders will agree with me, I control forty percent, so the majority will be on my side. We'll begin an orderly shutdown as soon as all the paperwork is done."

"I can't believe you'd use the shares I helped you buy from my mother to close down Dartmoor."

"You need to face facts. Closing down is what's best for Dartmoor, your mother, and you. I'd be derelict in my fiduciary duties to do otherwise."

The chill of failure seeped through her. "You haven't looked at the updated plan."

"The best plan in the world just puts lipstick on the pig, if the basics aren't there."

"That's what my plan does. It changes the basics."

His cell buzzed. He pulled it out and turned away from her.

"Hello, Astrid. I'm afraid I'm a bit behind here." He booted his laptop. "Let me get those files."

Defeated, for now, Madison left the office, carried his dinner in from the dining area, and set it on his desk. He smiled up at her for a moment, but Astrid must have asked him a question because he turned back to the laptop and started typing. A flashback of too many dinnertime phone calls her father hurriedly took into his den squeezed Madison's heart.

She ate what she could of the delicious dinner, added some soda to the whiskey glass, and sat at the piano, absentmindedly playing Mozart.

She wasn't entirely surprised at Jake's reaction. A chasm of distrust had opened between them since he'd seen the current numbers for Dartmoor. She couldn't really blame him. She should have checked the latest financials herself before Uncle Tyler sent them to him, but she'd been so wrapped up in working out the deal for her mother's shares, so eager to become Jake's wife and, frankly, so afraid of what she'd learn, that she hadn't bothered.

Once again she was paying for her cowardice.

She drained her glass. She wouldn't let Jake shut her out of the family business the way her father had. But forewarned was forearmed. She'd known Jake might brush off her attempt to change his mind, so she'd developed a Plan B. Now she needed to find the courage carry it out.

She'd worry about how to save her marriage after she saved her family's legacy.

Two days later Madison sat by the fifth-floor window of a department-store restaurant waiting for her lunch date. She unknotted her hands and spread her fingers on the soft navy wool of her suit skirt. The dark color and the tightly wound up-do she'd forced her hair into added a few years to her age, but that was to her advantage today.

If the Colonel ever showed up. She scanned the crowds on Market Street, as if she'd be able to recognize her grandfather's best friend among the swarming noon-hour shoppers below.

"Madison, darling." The familiar voice, raspy with age, came from behind her. "Don't you look lovely."

She turned and smiled up at the small, well-dressed man, who'd greeted her with the same words for as long as she could remember.

"How is your dear mother?" He took the chair opposite her and leaned the cane he despised against the window beside him.

"Same as always. How are you?"

He grimaced. "Old. How is married life treating you?"

"Well." Not exactly a lie. She and Jake had barely seen each other in two days.

The Colonel accepted a menu from the server. "So, to what do I owe the honor of being invited to lunch with you?"

She steepled her hands on the table. "I have a plan for Dartmoor…"

Lunch the next day was far harder, but Madison needed every vote on the Dartmoor Board she could get.

"How was the drive?" her mother-in-law asked her when the housekeeper showed Madison onto the deck where the elder Mrs. Carlyle sat watching the wind ripple the gray-blue water of San Francisco Bay. "Not too much traffic, I hope."

Rachel Carlyle was still beautiful, but her face was dimmed by grief. Empathy washed over Madison as she accepted a glass of Riesling from the housekeeper.

"Jake thinks I should move into the city," Rachel went on, "but I'm not ready." She gestured toward the Bay with her wine glass. "His father is out there somewhere. . ."

Madison started to say, "I understand," but she didn't.

No one ever suggested Rachel had loved her late husband, yet she was still clearly suffering from his death. Nothing she said or did indicated she would welcome more than a superficial response to her words, but Madison couldn't find the usual glib reply. Just before the silence became painfully long, Rachel sighed and turned to Madison.

"I hope you're not here to tell me you've left Jake again." A warm, but awkward, smile twisted her suspiciously perfect face.

Madison forced a smile in return. "Of course not. I'm here to tell you about the exciting ideas I have for updating Dartmoor Department Stores. As a former model, you'll see right away how the changes I have in mind can turn the business around."

"But Jake doesn't see it?"

Madison gave her a questioning look.

"You wouldn't need to sell me on it, if he did."

"He hasn't signed on to the concept yet, no."

"Do you expect he ever will?"

Tension tugged at Madison's smile. "He only controls forty percent of Dartmoor, so what he thinks isn't the final word. He doesn't understand women's fashion, not the way you do."

"Has he read your plan?"

A trick question, even if Rachel didn't know it. "We've discussed it at some length."

"Show it to me. I only own ten percent, but it might be time for my son to learn a thing or two about appreciating what he has before it's gone."

Madison's heart twisted at the words.

"Assuming it's a good plan, of course," Rachel continued.

Madison's smile came more easily. "It's a very good plan."

"What's wrong?" Astrid asked Jake when he suddenly shuddered in his chair.

"I. . .what's the expression? I felt like someone walked across my grave."

Astrid made a face. "Why do you say that?"

"Madison's having lunch with my mother today."

"How nice."

Suspicious, was what he thought it was.

He'd never told Astrid about the Dartmoor situation. He needed someone to talk with about it, but discussing his marriage with his assistant wasn't an option. Not after he'd seen the expression on Madison's face the other night when Astrid called.

Slowly he'd come to believe Madison really hadn't known what bad shape Dartmoor was in until he'd given her the numbers. None of it was her fault, any more than it was his. But she must be hurting. The rift between the two of them was only making things worse. He wished he knew how to help her through this, so she could settle into being his wife.

He should take her away somewhere, just the two of them. Leave Dartmoor and Carlyle's behind, turn off the cell, and convince her she had no reason to worry about Astrid, or any other woman. Convince her he wasn't anything like her father. Paris, maybe, or the Caribbean resort he was in negotiations to buy.

But right now he wasn't sure Madison would even agree to a trip with him. The question was how to get her into a more receptive mood.

"Hello, Jake, are you there?" came Astrid's amused voice.

He shook himself back to the present. "Sorry. Could you start again at the beginning? My mind wandered a bit."

"Seemed like your mind was more on a world tour."

She made a circular motion with her hand so the ruby ring

she'd bought herself for her birthday sparkled in the sunlight.

Inspiration struck.

"Say, would you do me a favor? When you go to lunch, pick me up a ring, or better a necklace from Tiffany's? Emeralds, I think. They'd match Madison's eyes."

Astrid's expression suggested he'd grown a second head. "You want me to do what?"

"Pick out a gift for my wife. It's in the PA job description somewhere."

"How much trouble are you in?"

He almost squirmed under her sharp gaze. "Enough."

"So you're going to spend thousands of dollars to fix it, but you can't be bothered to pick the gift out yourself."

"I don't have time to, um, shop." His flesh crawled at the mere word.

"Look, Prince Charming, do yourself a favor. Forget the ring. On the way home, go by a corner flower stand and buy the lady a gardenia."

"One gardenia?"

Astrid rolled her eyes. "When will men learn size doesn't matter?" She leaned in and tapped her fingers on the table in rhythm with her words. "Just do it."

Jake's hello kiss that evening when they met in the lobby of the San Francisco Opera House was everything Madison, or any wife, could wish for.

He immediately spoiled it by asking, "How was lunch with my mother?"

"Okay." She noticed the glass of whiskey in his hand. "Did you have dinner?"

"Astrid and I went out for sandwiches before my last meeting."

Madison shook off the now-familiar bite of jealousy. "You need a real meal."

He wasn't so easily distracted. "So, what did you and my mother

89

talk about?"

"Your father."

That distraction worked. His face clouded.

"Did she tell you. . .," he began, then stopped. "Was the sun out? The view from the deck is great when it's not socked in with fog."

"It was a gorgeous day."

Luckily the couple with season tickets for the seats next to theirs walked up to discuss this evening's opera, *The Temptation of Faust*. The irony of the title didn't escape Madison. With Jake's hello kiss still tingling on her lips, it was hard to justify the deal with the devil she'd been working on for the last few days. Save Dartmoor at the price of her soul. Or her heart.

Dartmoor had been on a downhill slide even before her father's death. Its demise might be inevitable. But more was at stake than her mother's family legacy and the jobs of their employees. Madison had something at stake, too – Jake's respect. If he'd listened to her latest ideas and explained why they wouldn't work, maybe she could have let it go. Only he'd brushed her off as if she was just a trophy wife after all. She wanted more. She deserved more.

Jake sighed. "It's nice to have one night off, at least."

"What?" The word came out harsher than Madison intended. "I thought you said you'd be home for dinner tomorrow. I had a special evening planned for us."

More than planned. She'd been counting on an evening at home together to make one last-ditch effort to get him to look at her new plan.

Jake must have misguessed what her plans were, because he wiggled his eyebrows.

"I promise to be home by bedtime, but Astrid and I will have to work late. I have the damned Dartmoor Board meeting all afternoon the next day."

So much for her last-ditch effort. Maybe it was for the best. If Jake refused to listen to her ideas one more time, she might have

90

to accept that more than Dartmoor was at risk.

The limo picked them up after the opera, but instead of going directly home Jake whispered to the driver, who made a detour to Union Square and pulled up at a flower stand. Jake hopped out of the car and returned with a single gardenia.

"A beautiful flower for my beautiful wife."

He'd said almost the same thing when he bought her a gardenia on their first date. Touched beyond words, Madison buried her face in the perfect white flower and absorbed its intoxicating scent.

When the limo drove away from the kerb, he kissed her and said, "Do you think Dartmoor could spare you for a week or so?"

That depended on which one of them came out of top at the Board meeting. The irony of the expression didn't escape her.

"I might be able to arrange it." She gave him a coy smile. "Why?"

"I was thinking we might have a belated honeymoon in the Caribbean."

"Us? Alone? Together?"

He laughed. "Is that one question, or three?"

"One." She cuddled closer, not convinced yet he meant it. He never took vacations.

"Yes, us, alone, together."

She sank into the warm pleasure of the idea. The trip could be a new beginning for their marriage after the Dartmoor Board meeting.

"I have to check out this resort we're buying, so I thought you might as well come along." His casual attitude tossed a bucket of cold water on her mood. "I won't be working all the time. If I am, we can stay a day or two extra. We'll sail, do some scuba-diving, check out the local restaurants."

At least he was making an effort. "It sounds lovely."

"You can buy some bikinis for the trip."

She rolled her eyes. "I have plenty of bikinis."

"Maybe one of those thongs. . ."

She swatted at him playfully. "I'll wear a thong when you do."

91

"I may take you up on that."

The shift in mood led naturally to their bedroom once they got to the penthouse. He undressed her with a kind of reverence, laid her on the bed, and made long, slow love to her until she was nothing but light and air in his arms.

"I love you," she whispered when she floated back to reality, but he was already asleep.

"Seriously, my mother talked about my dad the other day?" he asked her over breakfast the day of the Board meeting.

Her mouth full of Mrs. Lee's to-die-for Belgian waffle, Madison nodded.

"She doesn't talk about him with me."

"She didn't say much. Just sort of referred to him."

Jake scowled at the *Wall Street Journal* on the tablet computer in front of him.

"You didn't talk about Dartmoor? Why my dad bought those shares, I'll never know."

"My father talked him into it because my cousin needed to raise cash for the cooking school he was opening."

Jake slid his untouched plate toward Madison and stood. "I have to get to the office early. Damned Dartmoor meeting eats up half my day. At least there won't be many more of them."

She bit her tongue on a warning she didn't dare give him.

"You coming to the meeting?" he asked

"No." As CEO of Dartmoor, it would be better if she wasn't there. Uncle Tyler could vote her shares.

Jake gave her a ritual kiss on the cheek. "See you this evening."

"Er, I'm having dinner at my mother's." She planned to stay safely away from the penthouse until Jake calmed down after the Board meeting.

"Oh. Well, goodbye then."

Madison blew him a kiss, then reached for his waffle.

The condemned woman ate a hearty meal.

Jake walked the few blocks along the Embarcadero from the penthouse to Carlyle & Sons' headquarters, unease prickling up and down his spine. The unwelcome sensation became a chill when he realized Madison never answered his question about whether she and his mother had talked about Dartmoor.

"You look like a man who skipped breakfast," Astrid told him a few minutes later when she walked into his office. "I'll get you some donuts from the break room."

"I don't need donuts," he growled, but instantly regretted the display of bad temper. "I guess I do. Sorry."

"No problem." Astrid laid a one-inch-thick pile of papers on his desk. "Here's the Dartmoor Board meeting packet. Nothing out of the ordinary on the docket."

He didn't consider shutting down a business that had been in operation for over a hundred and fifty years "ordinary", but Astrid would. The enterprise was losing money, so it was time to let it go. Easy for someone as focused on the bottom line as she was.

"Focus on the bottom line," was what his father always said, too, quoting Jake's grandfather. Maybe Granddad should have added a few words about happiness and kindness. Then Jake's father might not have jumped off his sailboat in the middle of San Francisco Bay when the company hit hard times.

Jake's heart clenched at the memory, the loss. Not for the first time, he wished his father was alive to see how he had pulled Carlyle's back from the brink and made it one of the largest privately held companies in the state. Hell, he just wished his father was still alive.

Yup, he needed a donut. He had a hard day ahead and no dinner with Madison to look forward to at the end of it.

"Here you are." Astrid set a French donut and a maple stick in front of him and poured fresh coffee into the "World's Best Boss" mug she'd bought him as a gag gift for Christmas.

He and Astrid could have dinner together.

Nope. He didn't want to give Madison any reason to think his relationship with Astrid was more than strictly business. His wife hid her jealousy pretty well, but he knew her better than to buy the feigned indifference. Her suspicions had absolutely no grounds in reality, but given her father's reputation as a philanderer, he didn't blame Madison for expecting the worst of men. Still, her distrust only added to his doubts about why she'd married him.

He bit into the maple bar. The greasy sweetness eased, but didn't erase, the prickle along his nerves.

Once he got through this meeting, he'd take Madison to that resort and convince her to forget Dartmoor and focus on being his wife. He longed to come home in the evenings and have her to talk with about his work, instead of having to fend off her endless attempts to sell him on her ideas for saving a sinking – hell – an already sunken ship.

The thought that she'd be bored to tears staying home all day danced through his mind, but he relegated it to the mental trash bin along with the thought that followed – he'd be bored with her inside of a year, too, if she stayed home.

No. He'd never be bored with her. She was the most important thing in his life.

Not that he'd let her know that any time soon. He'd lived with his parents' tragically one-sided marriage too many years. He refused to play second fiddle to Dartmoor in Madison's life.

Too edgy to go to the office, Madison spent the morning moving the last of her things into Jake's penthouse. That done, she'd settled at the piano to play Chopin when the phone rang.

She jumped. Her stomach jumped higher, lodging in her throat.

She crossed the room and picked up her cell from the end table to check the caller ID, praying it wasn't Jake. She wouldn't know what to say to him.

With a sudden, painful clarity she saw what she'd done as the blackest betrayal. That she'd done it for her mother's sake paled in comparison like candlelight in the sun.

Dartmoor's sad state wasn't her responsibility. Maybe she should stop trying to clean up her father's mess and admit he'd failed them all.

Jake was right, her mother would do fine if they had to close the stores. Their employees would find other jobs, better jobs. Jake, on the other hand, was her husband. More, he was the man she loved. He deserved to come first in her life.

She was so stunned by that new reality she took a moment to recognize the number on her phone. Uncle Tyler.

She sagged against the back of the sofa and looked out the window toward the Bay.

"Hello." Her voice quavered so much he asked if it was her. "Yes, it's me. What's up?"

"I thought I'd give you some warning."

She stood up straight again.

"Warning about what?"

"About the plan the Colonel and I came up with."

She listened in stunned silence as he explained.

"Pretty clever, huh?" he said when he'd finished.

"How nice of you, but. . ." She couldn't find the words to praise him for ruining her marriage or to condemn him for offering her what she'd always wanted most.

Unable to think clearly, she said, "I'm late for a hair appointment. Why don't you call me tonight? I'm having dinner with Mother. You can tell me how it turns out then."

How it would turn out was much too clear. She'd publicly humiliated Jake once. The Board meeting might constitute a much smaller public, but the plan Tyler and the Colonel had come up with still might mean the end of her marriage, even if that wasn't what they intended.

"Sure. You're a busy woman. Talk to you tonight."

She hung up, her eyes fixed on the vase from her office staff on the mantel. The red roses Mrs. Lee had put in it that morning seemed to blaze a warning. This on-rushing replay of her first wedding disaster could cost her far more than she'd thought.

She'd left Jake at the altar because he wouldn't let her be who she wanted to be, but their short marriage had taught her that, more than CEO of Dartmoor, she wanted to be his wife. Even if he hadn't yet said he loved her.

She needed to stop this crazy new plan. The Colonel would be on his way to the board meeting, and he didn't believe in cell phones, so she punched in Tyler's number with shaking fingers. Too late. Her cautious uncle had turned off his cell while he drove across the bridge.

She should have begged him not to do it before he hung up, but Uncle Tyler sounded so pleased with himself she hadn't been able to object.

She should have ignored her sentimental reaction to his news and faced facts. That was what Jake said she should do about Dartmoor. And what she'd failed to do again.

One of the facts she needed to face was that the "new plan," as her uncle had called it, would have made her wildly happy under any other circumstances.

And Jake knew that. If he thought she was behind it, if he divorced her because of what happened today, they were back to where they'd been when she'd left him at the altar.

Except she loved him so much more now she wasn't sure how she could survive losing him a second time.

She had to find a way to save her marriage, even if it meant the end of Dartmoor.

Chapter Eight

Jake had to wonder what was up when his mother swept into his office a few minutes before the Dartmoor Board meeting was scheduled to begin. She gave him the obligatory air kiss and perched on the edge of his desk.

"How was the drive?" he asked her. "You really should move to the City, you know."

"I know," she breathed out what might have been a genuine sigh. "The drive was lovely, but renting a limo for the day cost a fortune. I don't suppose Dartmoor pays for that kind of thing for its Board members."

"No. Besides, you have the money to keep a limo and driver full time, if you wanted to."

His mother shrugged. "I never go anywhere."

If he hadn't known better, he would have thought she was grieving his father. As it was, he didn't have a clue why she'd become such a recluse, or what to do about it. Better to focus on what he could control.

"What brings you here today?"

She studied her perfectly manicured nails. "Watching out for my financial interests."

"Why didn't you send me a proxy, the way you do for the Carlyle & Sons meetings?"

She looked up at him with eyes the same clear blue as the ones that met him in the mirror every morning. "Maybe I felt the need to get out of the house."

No way to argue with that. "Just don't allow sentiment to cloud your business sense."

"I don't have any business sense, which is why I give you my Carlyle's proxy. But I do have some common sense, which is more than you've shown lately."

Tyler Ellsworth and the older gentleman Madison called the Colonel arrived before Jake could ask his mother what she meant. Time for the meeting to begin. He herded his visitors into the boardroom next to his office.

Going through the routine items on the agenda was like waiting for the other shoe to drop – or a bomb to explode. Jake amused himself during the dreary financial report by considering which was the more apt comparison.

Once they got to new business, he let his bomb drop.

"Mother, gentlemen, Consolidated Department Stores has offered to buy Dartmoor."

The announcement earned him everyone's undivided attention. Even the Colonel shook awake with a start of surprise at finding himself there.

"Well, that does change things," the older man said, more to Tyler than to Jake.

Jake made eye contact with each of them around the table, silently defying them to challenge him.

"How much was the offer?" Madison's Uncle Tyler asked.

The figure Jake cited sent another silent shockwave through the room.

"I believe, darling," his mother ventured, "that the last time we talked you suggested the real estate alone was worth a million or two more than that."

Since when did she pay attention when he talked about money?

"Yes, but this deal saves us the liquidation costs and shifts the pension and other liabilities to Consolidated."

"So, shutting down or selling means roughly the same payout for us," the Colonel noted.

"Roughly, but selling keeps the Dartmoor name alive."

His mother's Cheshire-cat smile widened.

"It'll only keep the name alive until Consolidated rebrands the stores as part of one of their chains," Tyler objected. "And selling means the money we get for our shares is the last income we'll see from Dartmoor."

"You haven't gotten a penny from Dartmoor in over a year," Jake reminded him.

His mother raised her hand. "What about Madison's plan to turn Dartmoor around?"

How did she know about that? Jake didn't have time to figure it out now. He needed to focus on getting them to agree to the sale.

"Her plan might not be enough to do the job." He wanted to say flat out it wouldn't, but didn't want to alienate an undoubtedly pro-Madison audience he needed to win over. "Then you'd end up with nothing at all."

"There'd still be the real estate," Tyler threw in.

"And the liabilities. Plus the cost of liquidation." Jake rubbed his temple where a headache was forming.

"In other words, if we try Madison's plan and it fails, we'll be right back where we are now," his mother summed up.

"With a higher debt load – and without the offer from Consolidated," Jake countered. "If the real estate retains its current value."

"It might be worth more in a year or two," his mother pointed out, sounding almost as if she knew what she was talking about.

The discussion see-sawed after that, but the Colonel seemed persuaded they should sell and keep the Dartmoor name alive, at least for a while, without further financial risk. With his mother's vote, Jake would have his sixty percent. The headache began to ease and a grin of triumph tugged at his lips.

Then his wife strode into the room like an avenging angel, emerald-green eyes blazing. And wearing the sexiest red suit he'd ever seen. Clearly all bets were off.

A ripple of anticipation ran through the room as Madison walked in. Surprise, and the beginnings of anger, froze her husband's face into an icy mask.

She shouldn't have come. She had to come. It was the only way to stop Uncle Tyler and the Colonel from trying to make things better for her while making them far, far worse.

Her mother wouldn't want her to save Dartmoor at the expense of her marriage. Even if she did, Madison needed to live her own life, not her mother's. That was why she'd left Jake once. This time it was why she was willing to sacrifice a failing family business to stay with him.

She met Jake's frigid stare and smiled at him with as much love as she could, hoping he'd understand she was on his side. Before she managed to say anything, both Uncle Tyler and Jake's mother started to talk at once.

"You first, Rachel," Uncle Tyler said.

Jake's mother cleared her throat. "I was going to ask Madison to explain her plan for rescuing Dartmoor to us. Maybe she can answer some of the concerns Jake has about it, so we can make a more informed decision about whether to adopt her plan or sell."

Sell? Jake dropped his eyes. He'd found someone to buy Dartmoor? How had he done that? And why hadn't he told her? The answer was obvious – because he'd been afraid she'd be upset if the deal didn't work out.

Guilt overwhelmed her. While she'd been conspiring against him, he'd been doing his best to find a way for them both to win. She wanted to tell him what a fool she'd been, how much she loved him, but this was not the time or the place.

Her presentation popped magically onto the plasma screen at the far end of the room.

"Yes, explain it to us again," Uncle Tyler said.

He gave her a wink and came around the table to hand her the clicker for the slide show.

She couldn't refuse to run through the presentation. She didn't want everyone to know Jake had tried to sell Dartmoor without telling her. He'd probably thought of it as a pleasant surprise, but under the circumstances it would look more like he'd schemed behind her back. She'd done enough scheming for both of them.

A weak presentation, on the other hand, might help her, no, his, no, their cause. She went to the front of the room and turned to her small audience with a wobbly smile. If only Jake's expression wasn't so cold.

"I'd rather not repeat what you've all already heard."

Jake raised one eyebrow in surprise, but his face remained glacial.

"Why doesn't Jake point out the weak points," his mother suggested. "Then you can answer him."

Or not. His years of experience in business should make it easy for him to poke holes in what she proposed. All she had to do was act dumb. Since she'd just pulled the dumbest trick of her life trying to outwit him, it shouldn't be hard.

All eyes turned toward Jake.

Jake pinched the bridge of his nose to ease the throbbing pain building up in his head.

How did his mother know he hadn't looked at the latest version of Madison's plan?

"It isn't a question of weak points," he said. "It doesn't matter how good what Madison has come up with might be, er, is. The fact is, Dartmoor cannot be saved."

"If Dartmoor's in such bad shape, why does anyone want to buy it?" asked Tyler.

"Because. . ." Because he'd spent most of a week selling Consolidated on it, minimizing Dartmoor's cash-flow problems, highlighting the strategic location of the stores. "Because they have the resources to finance the changes needed to put Dartmoor in the black."

"And Carlyle & Sons doesn't?" his mother muttered.

He glared at her, and she glared back.

"In any case, we'd all like to hear about Madison's proposal," the Colonel said.

The situation went south completely after that. Madison fumbled around as if she wasn't familiar with her own ideas, but she ultimately answered every objection. Even his.

Her original plan was a good one, which was why he'd used it as the basis for his pitch to Consolidated. This one was better.

All the same, the Colonel was still frowning when Jake took over the meeting again.

"Thank you, Madison. As per our by-laws, we'll decide this with voting members of the Board present only. Your uncle has your proxy, so you're not eligible to vote at this meeting. You can wait out in the lobby, if you like."

"No!" She let the clicker clatter to the table. "You don't understand. I have to stay. I have to make sure. . ."

"Make sure your side wins? You've already done plenty to ensure that. I have no choice. It's in the by-laws. We can't vote until you leave."

"But. . ."

"It'll be fine, dear," his mother said.

Madison turned wide, teary eyes to Jake. Clearly he'd underestimated how much Dartmoor meant to her. Or maybe she hated to lose as much as he did.

"Please, Jake. There's a plot. . ."

"A plot to go behind my back and sell your plan to the Board? I figured that out a while ago. Now, will you please leave the room so we can carry on with our business?"

The expression on her face shifted. Her jaw tensed. She lifted her head, straightened her shoulders, and walked slowly past him.

Her Uncle Tyler and the Colonel exchanged smug smiles. Jake had the eerie feeling he'd missed something important. Whatever it was, Madison wasn't about to clue him in at this point. Maybe he shouldn't have been quite so harsh with her, but dammit. . .

She shut the door behind her with a light slam, which reverberated through the table, up his arms, and right into his grinding headache.

He called for the vote, not entirely surprised when his mother voted with the others to adopt Madison's plan rather than sell to Consolidated. At least the ordeal was over.

"Thank you." He managed a thin smile and gathered his papers.

"One moment." Tyler nudged the Colonel out of his usual semi-stupor. "I'd like to suggest this new direction for Dartmoor might call for new leadership on the Board."

Jake closed his eyes against the now-thunderous pain in his head. "I thought the majority shareholder served as Chair of this Board."

"It's been the custom, but the by-laws don't require it." Tyler couldn't quite meet Jake's eye as he spoke. "I believe we need leadership with a clear vision of the company's future, but also a connection to its past."

"I second the motion," Jake's mother chimed in. "Madison has an emotional investment in Dartmoor and, as CEO and Chair of the Board, she'd be perfectly situated to turn the company around."

Jake's mind spun. After all the hours he'd put in on the deal with Consolidated, this was how Madison rewarded him – another public humiliation. She didn't know about the deal he'd bartered, but still she'd gone behind his back, again, to get her way.

His thoughts flew so fast and in so many directions he lost track of the conversation. The next thing he knew Madison was Chair of the Dartmoor Board, effective immediately. The room fell into silence as the others waited for his reaction.

Before he could say anything stupid, Astrid appeared in the doorway.

"Almost done? The conference call with the developer of the resort we're trying to buy is scheduled for about two minutes from now."

Jake rubbed his temple again and caught a sympathetic expression on his mother's face.

"Are we done here?" he said wearily.

Everyone stood as if on command and began to file out.

"Good day's work, good day's work," the Colonel mumbled to Tyler as they went.

His mother left last. "Jake?"

"What?"

"I don't think Madison knew. . ."

Anger surged through his body, but he kept his voice even. "Madison knew enough."

His mother shook her head and walked away, but Jake didn't have time to worry why.

Madison was still shaking when she stepped into the noise and bustle of Montgomery Street and realized she'd come out on the wrong side of the Carlyle's building.

She should have stayed. She should have fought harder for a chance to make Uncle Tyler and the others see that, even if they didn't sell Dartmoor, electing her Chair of the Board wouldn't help save the company and might very well doom her marriage.

But when Jake ordered her out of the room, her temper had snapped. For just long enough for her to regret it, she'd decided if he wanted to play hardball, he deserved what he got.

She hailed a cab and directed the driver to her mother's apartment in Pacific Heights, using the slow trip through the traffic-clogged streets to pull herself together. Her mother didn't need to know how close Madison was to a total meltdown.

"I expected you for dinner," Dana said mildly after the housekeeper showed Madison into the apartment's living room, where her mother was reading a detective novel.

"Did Uncle Tyler call?" Madison asked, too upset for formalities.

"Yes, he called." Her mother's tone was funereal.

Madison sank onto the sofa. "So, they voted to sell. I'm sorry. I did my best."

Her heart ached over the loss of Dartmoor, but if Jake had won, he'd never learn about Uncle Tyler's plan. A surge of relief made Madison light-headed.

"I'm sure you did," Dana replied in the same hollow voice.

The housekeeper reappeared with two glasses of wine. Madison took a sip, grateful for the chance to get her bearings, then suppressed a grimace. Why was it that Jake's mother always remembered she didn't like Chardonnay and her mother never did?

At least the worst was over – she didn't have to be the one to tell her mother Dartmoor would be sold. While Dana was clearly unhappy about the outcome, she didn't seem grief-stricken. Unless she was still numb. Madison felt pretty numb herself.

If Jake's arguments were strong enough to win over the Colonel, and maybe even Uncle Tyler, selling was probably the best plan. The money they got for Dartmoor could be reinvested to maintain her mother's lifestyle. Nothing would be lost except her family's legacy.

And once Jake's temper cooled, she and he would be able to start over on their marriage.

Her mother's knuckles were white as she gripped her wine glass. "Apparently your best was too good."

Dread settled in Madison's stomach like a lead weight. "They did vote to sell Dartmoor, didn't they?"

Her mother shook her head. "Tyler said Consolidated Department Stores made them a decent offer. It was nice of Jake to try to save the Dartmoor name."

Consolidated? Madison was impressed.

"So they voted to use my plan to rescue Dartmoor?"

A shudder ran through her mother, as if the next words needed to fight their way out.

Madison's heart rocked in her chest as she waited for the other shoe to drop.

"They also made you permanent CEO. And Chair of the Dartmoor Board."

Uncle Tyler and the Colonel went through with it. Now she understood why her mother had trouble talking. Madison could barely breathe herself, much less form articulated thoughts.

"Didn't Tyler and the Colonel have any clue what this might do to your marriage? No," Dana answered her own question, "I don't suppose they did. Your father was right after all. He always said his brother was an idiot."

Madison took a slow sip of her wine, too many emotions flying around her head and heart to speak up in her uncle's defense.

"Tyler said he'd never seen Jake so angry."

But Jake never wanted to be Chair of the Dartmoor Board. Then it hit her. Jake's mother must have voted with Uncle Tyler and the Colonel both times.

Jake didn't like to lose, but worse, he'd see the fact that she went behind his back to win his mother's vote as more proof he couldn't trust her. What could Rachel have been thinking? She, of all people, would know what all this might do to their marriage. Madison cradled the wine glass in her hand and closed her eyes, rocking slightly back and forth.

Strangely, at the same time it felt as if her world was falling apart, part of her wanted to do a little dance of celebration because the Board not only believed in her enough to use her plan, but enough to make her Chair as well.

Her mother took a sip of her wine. "It's not that I don't appreciate all your work to save Dartmoor. It means everything to me, it truly does. I only wish Tyler could have left it at adopting your plan. That would have made Jake angry enough. I hate to think that saving Dartmoor might cost you your chance of a happier. . ." She blinked. "Of a happy marriage."

"Jake will be mad, but we'll work it out."

Dana gave her a doubtful look.

Madison wondered, not for the first time, why she always ended up reassuring her mother when she most needed reassuring herself. After her father died, it'd been Madison who met with his mistress and insisted she resign immediately as CFO of Dartmoor, Madison who'd taken over as CEO, Madison who'd come up with the idea of contacting Jake for help after they'd exhausted all their other options.

And how is that working out for you?

"You could decline to be Chair. Except that's what you've always wanted, isn't it?"

Trust a mother to know your deepest, most secret, desires.

"If I declined, it would seem as if I didn't have enough faith in my own plan."

Her mother took a contemplative sip of wine. "Tyler said Jake was furious."

"He's been furious with me before."

"He does have a temper, doesn't he?"

He wasn't the only one. If Madison had kept her temper when he ordered her out of the meeting, she might have been able to keep all this from happening. But anger had been easier to bear than the pain of his thinly disguised scorn.

"It'll be okay. I'm sure."

She wished she *was* sure, but her marriage was her problem, not her mother's.

"What's for dinner?" Madison asked, her tone almost painfully bright.

When Madison walked into the glass-and-stone foyer of Jake's condo building a few hours later, the leaden sense of dread inside multiplied by ten.

The ride to the penthouse, always slow, was endless. Enclosed in the elegant metal box, she felt as if she'd jumped head-first off the Golden Gate Bridge and was watching as the cold, gray water slowly came closer and closer.

Just when the tension became almost unbearable, the elevator whispered to a stop and hissed open.

She let herself into the penthouse and threw her purse on the hall table. Jake's briefcase wasn't there, but he often put it in his home office.

The ebony, copper, and white living area was cold and empty, the African mask over the fireplace vaguely menacing. With its top open, the piano she loved had become a great black bird of prey hovering over the city below her.

She checked the darkened office with its scattering of electronic blue lights, but no sign of Jake. She let out a slow breath.

She didn't know whether she was happy he hadn't come home or not. Facing an angry Jake didn't appeal, but if he wasn't here, where was he?

A picture of Astrid's heart-shaped, intelligent face flashed through her mind. Her heart cracked along a familiar fault line.

She went to their bedroom without turning on any lights. As long as she was alone, she might as well enjoy the nighttime view. With the fog lingering further west, the lights of the city spread like a fairyland at her feet.

She was halfway across the room before she noticed the smell of gardenias and whiskey in the air. Three of the white flowers floated in a crystal dish on the bedside table. A large, dark lump on the white-leather chaise lounge shifted. She gasped.

"So, you came home after all."

Jake's voice didn't seem to come from the chaise, but filled the air with a mixture of anger, pain, and something Madison couldn't quite name, which left her gasping for breath.

"You scared me," she said.

"You scared me, too. Why sneak around here in the dark?"

He wouldn't want to hear about the fairyland of lights, so she didn't answer.

"Or has sneaking around become a habit?"

"I didn't. . ."

"Didn't sneak? Did I miss the part where you told me you intended to marshal your father's cronies and talk them into helping you and my mother oust me as Chair of the Dartmoor Board? Not the kind of thing I'd easily forget."

Maybe the best defense was a good offense. "You're drunk."

"Unfortunately, I'm not. This is my first."

"I'm sorry." She took a step toward him.

When he lifted his head, she froze.

"Sorry I haven't had more to drink, sorry you accused me of being drunk, or sorry you plotted behind my back?"

"Sorry about Dartmoor."

"Don't be." The dark shape on the chaise shifted. "As you once said, love and business are games without rules. And you won. You did your homework, you talked to your people, you sold your plan. I didn't."

He gave her a long look, stood and walked in a wide arc around her to turn on the lights and close the curtains.

"Care to make it up to me, Madison?"

She blinked in the brightness and nodded.

He chuckled, then crossed over to the cheval mirror and moved it next to the chaise. "Let's see if you're as sorry as you say you are."

"What. . .what do you intend to do?" she asked.

"Me? Nothing." He sat back down in the chaise. "It's what I want you to do that's interesting."

A strange tremor ran through Madison – half fear, half desire.

"What do you want me to do?"

"Take your clothes off. Slowly."

Heart racing, but already aroused, she stared at him.

"Why?"

"You were in control at the meeting today, even when you weren't in the room. Tonight I want to be in control."

He'd set the mirror where she'd see herself undressing for him, the way she had on their honeymoon. She wasn't sure if the gesture was mocking or sentimental, but the tension in her chest softened into hesitant butterflies.

"What do you have in mind?"

"Not knowing is part of the game. If you're willing to play."

The sooner they put today behind them, the sooner they could get their marriage back on track. That fact, plus good old-fashioned curiosity, swept away the last of her reservations.

"As you wish," she said in feigned submission.

Jake raised an eyebrow but didn't object when she clicked on the lamp by the bed and turned off the overhead light.

The butterflies that had invaded her stomach took wing as she slid off her suit jacket and began to unbutton her black silk blouse. She paused after each button to watch his face shift by degrees from anger to desire, if not yet the warmth his eyes had held on their wedding day.

By the time she pulled the blouse open, her nipples were jutting through the black lace of her bra.

The ice in his eye didn't melt when she slid the sleek silk blouse from her shoulders and let it drop to the floor, but his gaze went laser-hot as she reached behind her to unzip her skirt.

She pushed the short red skirt down her hips so it pooled at her feet, then stepped out of it toward him, just out of his reach. He made a low sound deep in his throat. The butterflies in her belly were in full flight now, diving down to tickle the hot, damp flesh between her legs.

She hesitated before she tugged down the black silk half-slip. She held it a moment, swinging in front of her before she turned at the waist and dropped it behind her.

She stood in front of him in black lace bra and panties, thigh-high hose she'd put on to boost her confidence for the board meeting, and high-heeled black sandals. She looked into the mirror, feeling like an Amazon. Reluctant to give up the height, she bent to undo her shoes.

"Leave those on." His voice was gruff as he gestured at the sandals and hose. He pointed to her bra and panties. "Take those off."

She reached behind her to unhook her bra, but held it to her chest with one hand as she took the straps, one at a time, from her shoulders. Finally she let it drop, freeing her breasts with their telltale budded nipples. The mirror reflected the dark-pink flush of arousal spreading across her white skin. Fascinated, she stroked her fingers across her chest, then tweaked a nipple.

Jake moaned again and she smiled. He was in control more than he knew, but she'd find as much pleasure as she could in playing his game. And apparently there was a great deal of pleasure to be found.

The panties would be hard to shed gracefully. She embraced the necessary wiggle, exaggerating it as she inched the tiny scrap of lace over her hips. She didn't drop it, but continued to glide it down her legs before she stepped out of it.

Uncomfortable with her naked reflection in the mirror, she focused instead on the rapt, vaguely tortured look on her husband's face. She waited, almost unbearably aroused, but with an edge of fear that only grew as he sat perfectly still, staring at her.

Chapter Nine

Jake had asked Madison to strip for him as a payback for what she'd done. But apparently she didn't consider stripping for him a form of punishment. In fact, she seemed to be wildly turned on by doing as he told her.

He was just as turned on, his whole body tense with need, his heart pounding. For a moment his brain swirled with the erotic possibilities, nearly drowning him with desire before he managed to pull himself back to reality. He swallowed. Her sexy smile broadened.

Once he had his impulses under control, he got up and stood behind her. The reflection showed the surprise on her face – and the wariness.

He stroked the tender skin of her neck. Her eyelids shut as she leaned into the caress. He traced a path across her shoulder and down the length of her arm. She shivered and he barely suppressed an answering tremor in his own body. Then she opened her eyes, still wary. Good.

He put his arm around her and drew his spread hand sideways across her belly so his thumb grazed the sensitive flesh under her breasts while his fingers traced the tender skin below her navel. The nerves jumped and she drew a sharp breath. He hid a smile in her shoulder and planted a kiss there, followed by a gentle nip that made her gasp again. Suddenly he took her bare breasts in both hands. Her eyes went wide.

"Yes," he murmured in her ear. "I want you to watch what I do to you."

She started to protest, but he caught her nipples between his fingers and she gave a low moan instead.

This time he didn't hide his smile as he teased and taunted the rosy nubs of flesh until her hips began the same tantalizing wiggle as when she'd slipped off her panties. He lowered one arm to press her hard against him so she'd know exactly how he was reacting to her. Her body quivered in his arms and he laughed.

Imagination running hot, he held both her slender wrists in one hand at her shoulder to pin her helpless as his other hand explored her naked body.

"Separate your legs," he growled.

Madison hesitated, wary again. Jake put his free hand on the inside of her bare thigh. Her legs melted apart, as if she no longer had any say in what she did.

When his fingers dipped into her moistness, her lids drifted shut and she rolled her head back on his shoulder.

He stopped. "You have to watch."

She lifted her head and blinked to keep her eyes open. The mirror reflected the dark slash of Jake's sleeve across her body, the ruby and gold of his cufflink, his tanned skin against the white of her belly as he explored her most sensitive flesh.

Finally he parted the delicate folds and touched the very center of her desire, and she began to tremble. He stopped, his smile wicked in the mirror.

"Say please," he prompted, then stroked one more time.

She saw the tension of unrealized fulfillment on her face in the mirror, his hand as he started to pull it up, his dark smile. He knew he'd won, damn him.

As his fingers slid away, her body convulsed in frustrated need.

She sighed and surrendered to the inevitable. "Oh, please."

His wicked smile widened and he caressed her until she fell over the edge into a tumultuous climax. When she went limp in his arms, he drew his hand slowly up her body, stopping to caress her breasts and she couldn't suppress another soft moan.

He swung her up in one swift movement to carry her to the bed, where he dropped her unceremoniously on the red silk duvet. His expression as he looked down at her made her reach to cover herself as she lay sprawled there.

"Don't move," he warned her, still staring at her naked body in a way that burned and chilled her at the same time.

Jake let the wave of tenderness he felt when Madison came apart in his arms flow over him until it threatened to wash away the last of his anger. But he wasn't ready to forgive her yet.

Once his breathing was back to normal, he reached down and lifted her ankle. She quivered at his touch, eyes wide, but he merely undid her sandal, drew it off her foot, and dropped it to the floor. He did the same with the other sandal, leaving her legs more widely spread.

He watched her watch him as he untied his tie. After a few moments she started to pull her legs together, but he stopped her with a raised eyebrow and she let them fall apart again.

Her willing vulnerability seared him, inside and out. He sucked in a deep breath for control before he undid his cuffs and unbuttoned his shirt. Belt, button, zipper and he was almost free. He'd taken his jacket, shoes, and socks off before she got home, so it was a simple matter to rid himself of his trousers and lay them on the chaise with the jacket.

As he did so, he glanced in the mirror and caught her eying his backside, the tip of her tongue visible between her lips. With a silent chuckle, he blessed the gym gods, then turned to stare down at her while he bared himself.

She wriggled her legs further open, and he could taste the

sweet victory.

Madison had heard that the brain was the most important sex organ, but she'd never quite understood what it meant.

Now she did. Watching Jake undress was sexy, but not nearly as sexy as the pictures of what he might do next that flooded her overheated mind.

Power was a dangerous game. She'd never expected the gamble she took to save Dartmoor to end up in their bedroom, with very different stakes.

She was willing to play Jake's game, but nothing in her nature made it easy. He wouldn't hurt her physically, but if he stopped at this very moment and walked out, she wasn't sure she could ever recover from the wound.

The darkness in his eyes told her he knew the power he had over her. She'd allowed him to lead her into a sensuous trap that left her almost unbearably vulnerable to his acceptance of her acquiescence in his game – or his contempt.

Was it all part of his plan, part of his revenge? The cold of doubt crept from her heart downward to her core.

Refusing to submit to it, she raised up on her elbows, legs still spread wide.

"Not even one kiss?" She smiled defiantly up at him.

With a deep, feral sound he all but leapt onto the bed, hands on her shoulders to push her down on the duvet. "Only one."

He kissed her – hard, incredibly hot. Tongues tangled, teeth nipped, until she couldn't tell who did what to whom anymore, so completely were they welded by shared need.

When he broke away, he paused to look down at her ravaged mouth. Then he was on top of her and all rational thought ceased.

He waited, poised at her center, his gaze fixed on her face.

"Yes." Her voice was soft this time, welcoming.

He entered her with a single thrust and raised himself over her, head thrown back like some primal beast.

The need her earlier climax had only fed exploded in a burst of joy and light. She cried his name as wave after wave of pleasure swept her further and further into the stratosphere. She was so lost in ecstasy she scarcely heard him call her name in turn as he poured himself into her. She shuddered and trembled with fading delight, falling into oblivion.

She could easily have slept all night, but after a blissful few minutes cradled in Jake's arms, he released her, rolled away, and got out of bed, ignoring her muted cry of protest.

He left the room still naked and probably still angry.

Groggily, she pulled herself up to sitting and piled the pillows against the bare wooden headboard so they could talk once he returned.

Which she hoped would be soon. She yawned and blinked her eyes to fight off the urge to lie down, bury her head under the duvet, and pretend it all never happened.

But that was exactly what was wrong with their marriage – they made love and fell asleep instead of talking to each other.

Not tonight. Tonight they'd talk and she'd do her best to ease her husband's anger and make up for what she'd done. She loved him too much to do anything else.

She heard him in the kitchen opening the fridge, then the whirr of the microwave. She crossed her fingers he'd bring the food into the bedroom to eat. She'd turned the lights on, so he'd know she was awake, and the cool metal chairs in the breakfast nook didn't invite naked dining.

Score! She thought a little wildly when he wandered in a minute later with a plate of left-over Chinese take-out and a bottle of spring water.

He gave her an uneasy look, sat on the bed as far from her as possible, and started to eat, the spicy aroma of the food mixed with the lingering scent of sex giving the familiar room an exotic atmosphere. He'd be in a better mood with a full stomach, so she let him wolf down several bites of his reheated dinner. Besides, she

116

didn't quite know how to begin what might be the most important conversation of their brief marriage.

It wouldn't help to say she was sorry again, so she tried, "Thank you."

He set down his fork, eyes hooded. "For what, teaching you about kinky sex?"

She cringed at his reduction of such a soul-searing experience to the lowest possible denominator, but soldiered on.

"Thank you for trying to sell Dartmoor to Consolidated."

"So Uncle Tyler told all, did he?"

"It was really very nice of you to make the effort to save the Dartmoor name." She tried to keep her tone casual. "Mother was very touched."

"I like your mother. She deserves better than she got from your father. Hell, you deserve better than you got from your father. You even had to marry me because he and his mistress ran the damned family business into the ground."

"I didn't have to marry you. We'd have found some way." She took a deep breath. If ever there was a time to go all in, this was it. "I married you because I love you."

He brushed the confession away as if it was so much confetti, and swept the one hope left in her heart away with it.

"You said the same thing three years ago, and I ended up stranded at the altar in front of a church full of people."

"I've explained why. I wanted to get my MBA." She swallowed. "You'd made it clear I couldn't do that and be your wife at the same time."

"What do you need with an MBA?"

"As it turns out, I'll need it to run Dartmoor."

Definitely the wrong time for sarcasm. Anger exploded across his face. He set the plate down, stood, and pulled his robe off the hook on the door.

"It served you well enough today. You're now Chair of the Dartmoor Board." He gave a mocking little bow.

"A job you never wanted," she pointed out.

"No, but I like to choose which jobs I take on." His face darkened. "And when I step down from them. But this was your goal all along, wasn't it? I was only a pawn in your game."

Madison forced air past the leaden weight in her chest. She couldn't deny she'd always dreamed of being Chair of the Board – someday. Still, it was one thing to admit it to her mother, another thing entirely to admit it to the man she'd replaced in the position. The man she loved, even if he had just thrown her love back at her.

He seemed to take her silence for agreement. "Your plan was pretty impressive. The update was better. Wish I'd seen the second version before I pitched the deal to Consolidated."

"What?"

He looked at her sharply, as if he'd realized too late what he'd said.

"You used my plan, the plan you said wasn't good enough to save Dartmoor, to sell it to Consolidated?" She hated the wobble in her voice, but she kept her head high, her eyes on his.

"Consolidated had the money to put your ideas into action. Dartmoor didn't." He looked down. "I wanted to keep the Dartmoor name alive, for your mother. And for you."

She waved his protest away with a gestured that echoed his dismissal of her declaration of love.

"My plan," she repeated. "You used my own plan to try to sell my family's business out from under me."

"I was trying to do what was best for you."

Pain and anger fought a short, epic battle. Anger won.

"Who are you to decide what's best for me? I'm perfectly capable of making my own decisions. But you still don't have a clue. You'd say anything, do anything to prove you're in charge. Even steal my ideas to use against me."

"Damn it, Madison. . ."

"Don't you swear at me, you unspeakable bastard! Get the hell out of my bedroom."

This last word came too close to a sob, so she stopped and waited, hoping he didn't see the shiver of suppressed tears that ran through her body.

Silently he walked out.

Now what? Jake carried the fresh glass of whiskey he'd poured into the guest suite and stared down at the fog creeping over the city.

He'd been so moved by Madison's reaction to his erotic revenge he'd nearly forgiven her for what she'd done, despite her final defiant gesture, daring him to take her. And that kiss, lord, that endless kiss

Yet, after the most intense sexual experience of his life, when he'd let the truth slip out and she'd turned on him, all the anger and pain inside spilled out again.

Which left him where? In the guest suite for the foreseeable future, if she had her way.

But the room she slept in wasn't her bedroom – it was his. If she didn't want to share a bed with him, she could sleep in the guest bed.

He'd march into the room and tell her so, asleep or not. He took another drink of the whiskey for courage first.

Maybe he'd wait until the morning to confront her. He got into the cold, empty guest bed and let the soporific mixture of great sex, vented anger, and strong alcohol take over his brain.

Now what? Madison laid a hand on the cold pillow on Jake's side of the bed as the dull glow of morning sunlight through fog filled the room.

She saw so clearly what she hadn't seen in the fury of her temper tantrum last night. Yes, Jake had used her own plan to go behind her back and pitch Dartmoor to Consolidated. But she'd gone behind his back to garner votes on the Board. So far, it was a tie in their little game of – what did he call it? – sneaking around.

The problem was, she'd done it for Dartmoor. He'd done it for her. He won. She lost.

Almost numb with the pain, she wondered if it would have hurt more or less to have him walk away the night before, in the moment when she knew he'd been considering it, before they made love.

No. For all it might cost her, at least she had the wonderful, horrible memory of a surrender so deep she'd come close to losing herself entirely.

She probably should be grateful he'd stayed angry. If they'd cuddled afterwards, saying impossibly sweet things to each other, she'd have done whatever he asked, Dartmoor be damned. Worse, he'd have known it. This way her dignity was more or less intact.

And she was Chair of the Dartmoor Board. A tiny thrill of excitement ran through her, in spite of what it had cost her.

She glanced at the clock. Nine a.m. Jake should be safely at work. Unless he was waiting for her with an apology. She gave a bitter laugh at that unlikely possibility and rolled out of bed.

Her clothes lay scattered across the carpet, but his were gone. A chill ran through her.

He'd have needed to come into their room to get clothes for work. What else had he done while she slept, drugged by tears and good sex?

She took a deep breath before opening his closet. It wasn't empty, but several suits and half the shirts were gone. There were gaping holes in the usually neat ranks of his tie rack.

She tensed against the pain and went to his dresser. His sock and underwear drawers were half empty. The leather box where he kept his cufflinks and watch wasn't there anymore.

Her husband had moved out of their bedroom. The fact that she'd ordered him to only made it worse.

She crawled into bed and let the racking sobs consume her.

She was stirred out of a desolate stupor some time later by a tentative knock on the door.

"Yes?"

"A Mr. Cochrane is on the landline," came Mrs. Lee's voice.

"Said you weren't answering your cell phone."

Cochrane's name cleared her brain in a hurry. The Dartmoor COO must have heard what happened at the Board meeting yesterday.

Madison rubbed achy eyes. "Please tell him to call me on the cell in five minutes."

She got out of bed and did the only thing she could do – start living the rest of her life.

It was closer to fifteen minutes before she was put together enough to face the housekeeper with a fake smile in place, even if still red-eyed and in her bathrobe.

"I have a cold," she told Mrs. Lee, who made a non-committal noise.

There were two calls from Cochrane, never a patient man, on her cell, and four from her mother. Business before. . .family. She dialed Cochrane first.

"Your housekeeper said you weren't feeling well," he said in lieu of a greeting.

Mrs. Lee had just earned her salary for the week.

"I hope you're not too ill to discuss business."

"No, I'm fine," Madison replied. "A slight cold. What's up?"

"I wish I knew. Got a call from your husband this morning. He told me I should talk to you about some major changes at Dartmoor."

She'd taken the cell to the living area. Now she sank down on the sofa, heart pounding at the mention of Jake.

"Why don't you and I meet. . ." she glanced at the time, "at two and I can go over the plan the Board adopted with you? Are you free then?"

"I can be."

The tantalizing smell of coffee drifted in from the kitchen.

"One more thing," Cochrane said.

"Yes?"

"What should I tell our people?"

Our people. Pride straightened her spine and warmed her heart.

"Tell them not to worry. Not only will Dartmoor solve our financial problems, we'll come out of it better and stronger."

Madison clicked off the cell with a hand that wasn't quite steady. Since when had she started channeling her father?

She went into the breakfast nook to find not only coffee but a Belgian waffle with fresh strawberries. A contented sigh found its way past the emptiness where her heart used to be.

Mrs. Lee walked in as Madison sat down.

"Thank you. This looks great," she told the housekeeper.

"Mr. Carlyle said he wouldn't be home for dinner." Strawberries and whipped cream became dust and ashes. "Should I leave a meal for you?"

"No. I have to go to the office. I'll stop for take-out on the way home."

Madison saw no reason not to dress to please herself. If white linen pants and a brightly flowered silk blouse offended Cochrane's sense of business decorum, she'd hire herself another COO. She shook her head at the thought while she tied her hair back with a scarf that caught the emerald green in her blouse. One last check of her make-up and she was ready for duty number two of the day. She settled on the sofa and pushed her mother's number on her cell.

Ten minutes later she clicked the phone off, closed her eyes and laid her head back on the sofa pillows. Lying always exhausted her, but her mother was finally convinced all was well with her daughter's marriage.

As if. But Madison didn't have time to worry about the disaster that was her personal life. She needed to begin the hard work of saving Dartmoor.

She checked the time. Nearly one! She rushed to the kitchen to down an energy bar and another cup of coffee, then grabbed her computer bag so she could update the presentation in the car, and had the doorman call the Carlyle limo while she rode down

122

in the elevator.

Luckily, the Golden Gate Bridge wasn't too backed up, so she reached the Dartmoor headquarters with enough time left to make her usual stops on each floor to greet the staff.

When she finally reached the office suite on the top floor, she and Cochrane drafted a reassuring email about the changes to send out to the rank-and-file employees and a more detailed follow-up to the minimal message he'd already sent around to the leadership team.

After they were done, she opened the presentation on her tablet. She hoped she didn't look as nervous as she suddenly felt. A minute ago she'd been Charlie Cochrane's boss as they solved a business problem together. Now he was someone she needed to buy into her ideas.

She took a deep breath and plunged into the explanation of the plan, well-rehearsed by her meetings with Uncle Tyler and the others. Cochrane listened with the same impassive expression as her uncle and posed many of the same questions. Then he shuffled through the hard-copy pie charts and sketches with an occasional nod or frown.

"Why didn't you run this by me before?" he finally asked.

"I didn't want anyone at Dartmoor to know about it until the Board approved it, so no one built up any false hopes."

"Will your husband or his company put up the money for all this?"

Even the indirect reference to Jake almost robbed her of the breath to answer.

Luckily, she'd put the long ride over in the limo to good use. "You'll have to get our finance people to work up an exact budget for the changes, but based on the figures you see here, I'm reasonably sure we'll have access to enough private capital without Carlyle's involvement."

If nothing else, she could add what little money she had left from her grandmother's trust to the money Jake had paid her mother for her shares and build from there.

Cochrane's round face split into a grin. "You know, I think it'll work. Why don't we see if we can gather the whole leadership team together for their input?"

"Of course. This is only a preliminary sketch. If everyone likes the concept, the marketing, buying, and finance departments can start in on the details."

He looked at her for a moment. "I came up in Dartmoor, you know. I knew your grandfather. And, I have to say, you remind me of him. A lot. And that's a very good thing."

She gave him a wobbly smile and blinked away the sting of tears.

Madison was still basking in the afterglow of the Dartmoor leadership team's enthusiasm for her plan when she got into the limo to go home four hours later.

She'd seriously considered accepting Charlie's invitation to a celebration dinner, but the Carlyle driver was supposed to be off duty at six. He wouldn't be, but he'd be free before it got too late, now rush hour was almost over.

She checked her cell for messages. One. From her mother. Madison hit "call."

"Where are you, dear?"

"On the way home from San Rafael."

"Not driving?" her mother asked in alarm.

"No, I took the limo."

"Jake's limo?" Her tone, the mere mention of Jake's name, put Madison on edge.

"The Carlyle limo, yes."

Her mother let out a long breath. "I'm so relieved you and Jake worked it all out."

No reason to spoil her mother's day with the truth.

Ten minutes of chit-chat later, Madison clicked off the call and scanned email on her cell.

No messages from Jake. She laid her head on the sleek leather upholstery.

No way not to go back to their empty penthouse. If Madison went to her mother's apartment, Dana would suspect something was wrong. So would Jake's mother. It was a sign of true desperation that Madison had even thought of her.

The first night of the rest of her life. She ignored the sting in her eyes and turned the sound system to a classical station. Schubert's *Unfinished Symphony* drifted through the air. She allowed herself a moment to appreciate the irony of the title before she surrendered to the music.

Jake crunched the paper wrapper in his hand and tossed it with practiced ease into the wastebasket across the room.

"Always a good sandwich," he told Astrid, although he couldn't have said whether it was pastrami or ham.

"Let's call it a night," she replied. "We're all caught up, so I can leave with a clear conscience." She frowned at him, as if wondering whether his conscience was clear or not.

"But. . ."

"Jake, I don't know or care why you want to hang around here all night, but I have a date and I'd rather not have to go in my work clothes."

"Okay. Good night," he mumbled as she left.

Nothing to do but go home. Maybe he'd stop at a bar on the way. Or two.

He wasn't drunk, he gauged, as he rode the elevator to the penthouse two hours later, nor did he feel any better, but at least he might be able to sleep.

The penthouse was dark and silent, but Madison's purse was on the hall table and her cell was charging in his home office.

He sniffed the air. She'd brought home Thai food for dinner. His stomach growled. He opened the fridge in hopes of leftovers from her meal, but no such luck.

He took out bread, ham, lettuce, and mustard, but by the time

125

the sandwich was made, he'd lost his appetite. He ate the tasteless blob anyway, and realized it'd been a ham sandwich he'd eaten for dinner, too.

He was cleaning up the kitchen when the thought hit, robbing him of air. What if Madison wasn't asleep?

He went down the hall. No light under the bedroom door, no sound from the room beyond. He lifted his hand to knock.

What would he say to her?

Charlie Cochrane had called late in the afternoon to re-verify that he should go ahead with Madison's ideas for Dartmoor, raving about how enthusiastic everyone was about it.

"Great idea, adopting Madison's plan and making her permanent CEO as well as Chair of the Board," he'd said. "Great idea."

Not news Jake was about to share with Madison. Not yet, anyway.

No, he'd kiss her awake instead, have her in his arms before she could protest. Once there, he knew from experience a protest would be the last thing on her mind. His body jolted to attention at the thought.

That was the whiskey talking. The only way he'd get back in her bed tonight was to grovel, and he didn't do groveling. Ever.

She'd ordered him out of their bedroom. He'd stay out.

Whether or not she had a right to be angry didn't come into it. He sighed and went on down the hall to the guest suite.

Chapter Ten

Madison made sure she was ready well before Jake was due home for dinner the next evening. She put bottles of his favorite imported beer in the fridge, took out a bottle of Cabernet, and filled the ice bucket in case he wanted whiskey.

She put on a green-silk halter dress that matched her eyes, then double-checked her hair and make-up. She considered leaving her feet bare, but remembered the rough edge to his voice when he'd told her to leave her sandals on the night of the Board meeting. She dug out the pair of strappy cream-suede sandals she'd worn to their wedding and put them on.

She had to know where she stood with Jake.

She sat down at the piano and tried to distract herself with Chopin waltzes, but hunger forced her into the kitchen about nine. She choked down some bread and an apple before the knots in her stomach made eating more impossible.

She was about to break down and call his cell at eleven o'clock when she heard his key in the front door. Quickly she slid her phone between the cushions on the sofa and did her best to put on a calmly expectant face.

He came into the room with the mail and frowned at her. "You still up? Don't you have an early meeting with Cochrane tomorrow?"

Her heart bucked in her chest. "You're very well informed."

"I can search your calendar online."

"Yes, but why would you?"

"To schedule an appointment to discuss Dartmoor before the next Board meeting."

Something ripped open deep inside her, leaving her torn and bleeding.

"Schedule a meeting? I'm your wife."

"I wasn't so sure anymore, so I thought I'd better play it safe." His expression held no clue whether he was serious or goading her. "I put the meeting down on your calendar for tomorrow afternoon. You were free then."

She brushed his icy tone away. "Where have you been?"

"I went to dinner at my mother's. I knew I'd get a warm welcome there, and a good meal." His mouth twisted in a humorless smile. "Mother wasn't overly pleased to see me, actually. Seemed to think I should be home with you. I didn't want to tell her you'd thrown me out of our bed, so I lied and said your stomach was acting up. She hopes you're better."

Madison's stomach was acting up. It'd been tied in knots for hours.

"You and I need to talk."

He looked up from the letters. "That's why I set up an appointment for tomorrow."

Before she could tame the jumble of emotions battling for control of her heart, he went down the hall. The door of his home office closed hard behind him, just short of a slam.

She refused to chase after him. She couldn't force him to talk to her any more than she could force him to love her.

Jake was up and in the office early the next day. Sleep had eluded him most of the night, as he tossed and turned alone in the guest bed and he wasn't ready yet to face Madison over breakfast. He spent the morning drafting the introduction for the annual Carlyle

128

& Sons financial report before forcing himself to eat another tasteless sandwich for lunch.

The first email he saw when he got back to the office was from Charlie Cochrane, an update on the steps they were taking at Dartmoor to implement Madison's plan.

"Don't bother with further updates," Jake replied. "You don't work for me anymore."

If an appropriate job came up, however, Jake would do his best to steal Cochrane away from Dartmoor. Show Madison how the big boys played the game. He smiled grimly.

Astrid walked into his office a while later to find him staring at his screen saver.

"Trouble in paradise?"

Jake shut his eyes, then opened them as he made a conscious effort to relax. "Headache."

"Poor man."

The gentle teasing he usually returned in kind rubbed raw nerves. His head was pounding like the bass drum in a high-school marching band.

Not taking oneself too seriously helped keep a man sane in the business world. But his marriage wasn't business, even if he might taunt Madison sometimes with the idea that it was.

The rift with Madison was slowly killing him. He'd probably been wrong to steal the plan she'd developed to make Dartmoor viable and use it to try to sell the company, but he needed to find a way to patch up his marriage without groveling. He hadn't groveled when she left him at the altar, despite the pain and public humiliation. Maybe because of them. He was back in the same place now, but this time he was old enough to know what he wanted – he wanted Madison.

"Earth to Jake, earth to Jake," Astrid said lightly. "Are you there, Jake?"

He gave his head a shake and winced at the jolt of pain.

"Do you want me to start reading this report from the top?"

Astrid asked with a sympathetic smile.

"Actually not. We can catch up on this later. Right now I need to rush over to Tiffany's."

Astrid groaned. "Not the buy-yourself-out-of-it approach again! You get points for intending to pick the gift out yourself, but trust me, it's not going to work."

Anger simmered, but he rolled his eyes as if it was all a joke. "Gardenias won't cut it this time."

"You can come up with something better, Prince Charming."

A memory from before the Dartmoor Board meeting rose to the surface of his mind.

"What if you contact the resort we decided to make a bid on and set up an on-site visit in the next few days? I'll take Madison along."

"Better. But are you sure mixing a work trip with a pleasure trip is a good idea?"

"Why not? I trust you to keep the accounting straight so Carlyle's doesn't pay for her expenses or the cost of an extra few days."

Astrid shook her head and went into her office. She was a real bean-counter, probably because her MBA was in accounting.

MBAs made him think of Madison. And now that he had a plan, thinking of Madison made him happy, not to mention sexually aroused. He reined in his body's reaction. He'd have to play it straight with her in bed for a while, let her take the lead, to make up for what he'd done the other night. He wasn't complaining. Any sex with Madison was good sex. Great sex.

After much dithering, Madison chose to wear a silver-gray silk wrap-around dress for her meeting with Jake. While perfectly suitable for the office, the fabric clung to her curves and the hem fluttered at her knees.

For the third time, she was caught between her love for Jake and her pride. The first time, pride won, and she'd gotten her MBA, but at a far higher price than she'd expected.

130

The second time, Dartmoor's financial problems had outweighed pride. She'd braved Jake's anger to ask for a loan and gotten a proposal of marriage instead. But the business reasons behind their marriage gave them a weapon against each other that, until the night of the Board meeting, neither of them had used.

Third time's the charm, her Grandmother Moore used to say. What Madison did, even what she wore today, could determine her future with the only man she'd ever loved, or ever would love. She hoped she'd find a way to salvage both her pride and their marriage.

But her pride wasn't the only issue here. She'd hurt Jake's pride, too, so she needed to start the healing process there. The trick was not to surrender her self-respect in the process.

She took a deep breath before she walked into Jake's office and closed her eyes, not quite in prayer, but wishing for luck.

Silently he gestured her to the conference table by the windows. Not an auspicious beginning. Once they were seated, he opened a file folder and turned on the laptop next to it.

"I need to transfer my Dartmoor files to you, now that you're Chair of the Board."

Her heart sank, but she held onto her smile and nodded. She went on nodding as he talked her through the papers in the folder and the computer records he'd send her electronically later.

Once he was done, she put the files into her briefcase and looked up. Jake stood at his desk, staring down at his computer. Now was the time to try to save her marriage.

She mentally reviewed the speech she'd prepared. She'd liked it better in the shower, but it would have to do. They couldn't go on like this, and they couldn't go back to the way things used to be.

As she was about to launch into the speech, Astrid stuck her head in through the door to her office. "Still here, Mrs. C?"

Madison hated the nickname instantly. It made her feel old enough to be Jake's mother.

And he was chuckling at it! How dare that woman make him

laugh?

The rupture in their marriage was making Madison crazier than she'd thought, dredging up memories of her father's many infidelities, of all the anger she'd buried away since his death.

She needed to focus instead on saving her marriage. If Jake would give her the chance.

"Can you come back in a half an hour?" he said to Astrid.

Half an hour? Madison's battered heart perked up.

His wife's lips twitched toward a smile when Jake told Astrid to leave. A good sign. Now to see if Madison was ready to go back to the way their relationship had been before this mess.

His gut tensed at the significance of what was at stake.

"Now we have our business done, I have a non-business question. Do you think Dartmoor can do without you for a few days?"

Madison looked wary, but didn't shift out of her receptive body language. "I suppose I could manage a few days. I've handed the plan over to the staff, and the outside financing is beginning to fall into place."

"Yes, so I heard."

Her eyes narrowed. "Cochrane is reporting to you?"

"I've told him it wasn't necessary anymore. Where'd you find the money?"

"We put all the money you gave Mother for her shares on the table to leverage financing from local governments eager to keep the stores open, and got loans from local banks. Dartmoor is an important anchor for the downtown shopping districts in several of the outlying suburbs."

He'd never have come up with that. Not surprising. He knew diddly squat about retail. The only source he'd thought of for financing the changes at Dartmoor was loans from Carlyle's.

"Nice work." He consciously relaxed face muscles that seemed determined to frown. "So, do you still want to take off to that Caribbean resort with me?"

Madison blinked in surprise. Then she remembered his suggestion of a trip before the Dartmoor Board meeting.

"Be there with you while you work?" She kept her tone neutral, clueless as to where the conversation was headed.

"And stay for a few days after I'm done, just you and me."

He grinned at her a little. Not a real smile, but much closer than she'd seen in what seemed like a very long time.

She beamed with relief.

"It sounds great."

Maybe they could talk about their marriage while they were there so they didn't fall into the same patterns. She refused to go back to being Jake's trophy wife, even if only in his mind.

"Good." He clicked his computer. "Leave Thursday, stay six or seven days?"

She nodded while she mentally rearranged her schedule. Nothing she had on her calendar was more important than this.

"Don't forget to buy a thong." His grin turned lecherous.

A hot wave of pent-up need coursed through her, arousing nerves and flesh already softened by relief. She looked into his eyes and saw an answering flash of passion.

"I'll be sure to buy one for you, too."

He crossed the room and scooped her up into his arms.

Sex instead of talking. But they had talked. Sort of.

His kiss was hard with hunger, but totally different from the punishing mockery of the last time he kissed her. She melted into his familiar strength with a murmur of delight. Caught between the flame generated by his embrace and the heat that burned down to her center from the friction of her beaded nipples against his chest, she arched her neck to give him fuller access to her mouth and her body.

He made an impatient sound and raised his head to maneuver them to the large leather sofa under the windows, where he laid her down and covered her body with his, claiming her mouth in an even more passionate kiss.

133

"Oh, I've missed this," he groaned.

And I've missed you. She let the twinge of uncertainty at the difference between their choice of words pass. She'd missed the physical bliss between them, too.

He stroked up under her skirt and down the sensitive flesh of her thighs, his need pressed against her belly. He nibbled down her neck, and she raised her body in silent invitation.

When he drew in a deep breath and sat up beside her, she gave a small moan of protest. He smiled down at her, filling her with unexpected joy.

He slid his fingers inside the vee of her dress to cradle her breast reverently in his hand. New waves of sensation left her hot, wet, mindless.

He teased the pulsating nipple nearly to the point of release, then repeated the delicate torture on its mate. She writhed under his erotic attention until finally he pulled her legs apart and lay between them, fumbling with his trousers.

"Bad time?" Astrid asked from the doorway.

Jake swore, resting his forehead on Madison's. "Get out!"

The door closed behind Astrid and he rolled to his feet, laughing. Laughing together was probably what Madison had missed most, almost more than sex.

Once they were both fully dressed again, he took her in his arms and kissed her lightly.

"Tonight," he whispered.

Little thrills of delight shimmered through her body.

Astrid knocked on the door and he went to open it.

"You should have knocked last time, you know."

"And missed all the fun?" Astrid replied with a giggle.

Madison felt her face heat as she gathered up her briefcase and made a hasty exit.

Her first meeting as Chair of the Dartmoor Board, held back at the flagship store in San Rafael the next day, was an undeniable success. In only a few minutes the Board authorized the updates in her plan, starting with the stores where local loans and government money were available, so her mother could invest part of her cash to generate immediate income.

At the end of the meeting, Jake produced a bottle of champagne and a corsage of gardenias to celebrate. She blinked away the sting of tears when they all toasted her success.

As the rest of the Board members were leaving, he poured the last of the champagne into her glass. "To the Caribbean."

She clinked her glass against his. "To the Caribbean."

They drank, looking into each other eyes. A white-hot need that had little to do with the wine began to glow in her body.

He kissed her as he took her glass. "I have to get back to Carlyle's for another meeting." He checked the time with a regretful smile. "Right now. Hold the thought until tonight."

Which gave her enough to think about while she went through the rest of the day that she kept singing happily to herself.

Madison woke the next morning with a dozen pleasant aches and a busy day ahead of her. Still, she managed to leave work early so she could pack for the trip. She was already done with that when her mother called. The housekeeper had asked for a few days off, so Dana was waiting for a friend to pick her up for a wine-tasting trip to Sonoma.

"Everything's all right between you and Jake?" she asked.

Madison was surprised to find herself hesitating before she answered. Of course everything was all right. Despite two nights of great sex, they'd still never talked about their marriage, but they could do so during their time alone together at the resort.

"Sure." She quickly told her mother about the trip to the Caribbean.

"What time do you leave tomorrow?"

Madison didn't know. She laughed about Jake forgetting to tell her, without quite saying what else he'd considered more important the night before. She used it as an excuse to say her goodbyes and called his office.

"Hi, Mrs. C," Astrid greeted her. "I'll email you details. I didn't do it before because I assumed the boss would fill you in. He and I leave early tomorrow in the corporate jet, but he said you didn't like the little plane, so I booked you a first-class seat through Miami. You'll get to the resort about dinner time. I bet you're looking forward to three days in the Caribbean."

"Three days?"

"The boss said you'd talked about staying longer, but I couldn't clear a whole week from his schedule without his direct say-so, and he's been too busy for me to ask. I think he'll have at least one evening free to spend with you, unless something important comes up."

Astrid clicked off. Madison stared at her phone until it beeped in indignation and disconnected itself. The noise roused her from her semi-stupor enough to let the edge of the anger and pain slice through her heart.

What she'd thought was as a romantic escape was just another three-day business trip to Jake. A business trip with privileges. Clearly, for him nothing between them had changed at all.

And Astrid would be there, too. The time alone that meant so much to Madison clearly meant nothing but sex to Jake. They needed to talk, not . . .

She put one hand to her chest as if to hold closed the ragged edges of her heart and let the rage take over. Her hand shook with anger as she wrote Jake a note telling him to have a good time with Astrid in the Caribbean. She left it on the dining table, picked up her purse and already-packed bag, and fled to her mother's apartment.

But the familiar space did nothing to calm her. She wandered from the windows overlooking the bay to the ones that looked out on a vibrant cityscape, remembering happier times she'd spent here after her Grandmother Moore had sold the big Mill Valley house and moved into the City.

The apartment had been a refuge then, too. A place where she could forget the nights her father didn't come home, the arguments, the icy silences, her mother's tears.

She'd never understood, would never understand, how her mother had lived with a husband who considered his marriage vows mere "guidelines." Madison was pretty sure he'd taken his first mistress while Grandfather Moore was still alive, before control of Dartmoor's was an issue. Maybe her mother thought she could change the man she loved, find a way to keep him faithful. Later must she have figured out what Madison had grown up knowing – cheaters cheat. All the love in the world couldn't cure what ailed her parents' one-sided marriage.

Madison wasn't sure love could cure what ailed her marriage, either. She needed to find a way to cope with the very real possibility it was already over.

No, she needed to *deal* with the possibility it was over. Coping wasn't enough.

She'd coped after leaving Jake at the altar. She'd buried herself in business school, aced every class, won every prize. She'd put her life on hold, waiting for Jake to show some sign he'd forgiven her. Even before her father's death, she'd been putting off companies that recruited her because she didn't want to commit to a future with no escape clause, in case Jake wanted her back. And now she was in that same lonely place, with no more idea of how to deal with it and move on than she'd had before.

Finally, she choked down some leftover lasagne from the freezer and watched an old movie until it got late enough to go to bed She lay in the narrow single bed in the same room she'd used as a girl, with its pink-and-green plaid wallpaper, and stared at the ceiling, her mind full of regrets about her past.

She wasn't even sure where to begin. When she left Jake at the altar? When she agreed to marry him the second time? When she went behind his back to save Dartmoor?

She drifted off before she could decide, but woke up with the answer clear as sunlight in her mind.

Her true regrets began yesterday, when she'd jumped to conclusions about the trip to the Caribbean without giving Jake a chance to explain. Without even talking to him.

She'd always thought her mother had too little pride, but maybe she had too much. Enough foolish pride to destroy her marriage.

She sat up and fumbled in the dark for the cell she'd put on the bedside table in the unacknowledged hope that Jake would call after he saw her note.

Six a.m. If the Carlyle jet's take-off was set for early morning, he might be awake.

Her fingers shook as she pushed his cell number.

And got an "in flight" message. Damn.

As the last wisps of sleep faded from her brain she remembered she'd never read the email Astrid sent with the flight information. Madison quickly scrolled down to find it.

She still had plenty of time to catch the plane to Miami. She threw off the covers and stretched, ready to do battle for the only thing that mattered in her life – her marriage.

One again, Jake's soft heart had screwed him over. He hadn't wanted to wake Madison by calling her when he got home at two a.m., or before the plane left at five-thirty. His sleep-deprived brain might have thought he could wait until after this trip to deal with whatever craziness had caused her to leave the nasty little note, but now he'd had a second three hours of sleep during the flight, he saw that plan for the gross stupidity it was.

He should have called her right away.

No, he should have gone to the damned apartment, where she was hiding, dragged her back to the penthouse, and made love to her until the outside world vanished completely for both of them.

The thought added a thick layer of sexual frustration on top of his other jumbled emotions that made it hard to consider a rational course of action. He shifted in his seat to adjust for the tightness in his trousers.

"You okay?" Astrid set aside her magazine. "Should we review the talking points again?"

"No," he barked.

She waited for the usual apology for his bad temper, but he couldn't forget her role in this whole fiasco. She should have consulted him before she changed his vacation with Madison into a strictly business trip. Of course, he should have checked on the arrangements himself, but he was in no mood to shoulder any of the blame.

"No, you're not okay, or no, we shouldn't go over the talking points?"

"Both."

"Not air-sick, are you?" She laid her hand on his arm. "It's kind of bumpy. . ."

He stared at the hand until she took it away.

"Sorry," he said, not sure what he was apologizing for. "How much longer 'til we land?"

Madison's stomach lurched whenever the island-hopper airplane jumped or swerved as the pilot flew through the second thunderstorm they'd encountered since Miami. She felt like applauding when he made a ragged landing after one aborted attempt.

Relieved to be on the ground, she accepted the rain that flattened her clothes to her body as part of the tropical experience and hurried with the other passengers to the terminal through the storm's artificial darkness.

Soon she was in a taxi speeding across the island, but she couldn't see more than the outlines of the luxuriant foliage along the narrow, rutted road.

Jake would need to add road repair to his budget for the resort, if he bought it, or provide a launch to take guests there by sea. The wealthy tourists he'd be bringing here would never tolerate the punishing bounces of the elderly cab.

By the time they reached their destination, the sky was clear and she was able to appreciate the serene beauty of the beach and faux-rustic buildings of the resort. The cabbie deposited her at the main entrance and headed back to the airport for another fare.

Wet and beyond bedraggled, she was relieved to find the only other people in the lobby were the bellman dozing in a corner and a bored-looking young woman behind the front desk.

"Do you have a reservation?" the woman asked.

"I'm here with my husband, Jake Carlyle."

The woman raised an eyebrow. "Do you have any identification?"

Madison handed over her passport, which the woman studied closely. Understandable, since Madison hadn't been soaking wet when the picture was taken. She shivered in the air-conditioned cool.

At long last the woman returned her passport, typed for a moment on the computer in front of her, then gave Madison a key card in a discrete paper folder.

"You're in the Presidential Bungalow. Maurice will show you."

Instantly awake at his name, the bellman appeared at Madison's side to offer a hearty welcome to the island, in sharp contrast to the young woman's bored disdain.

The main building of the resort was a large hotel, but a couple of dozen bungalows of various sizes spread out from it, connected by a maze of wooden walkways. Maurice led her down one of them and stopped at a bamboo fence to unlock the gate with Madison's key. On the other side, yet another walkway led to one of the larger bungalows.

"This bungalow has three bedrooms, two baths, spa tub, wet bar with a microwave, and plasma TV's downstairs and in the master suite."

Maurice's accent lent the stock description a poetic quality, but Madison didn't hear much of what came after "three bedrooms." Was Astrid staying here, too?

Maurice glanced at the dark building. "Guess your man ain't here."

Madison's heart thumped against her chest. The novel she'd read on the flight to Miami, flying through the storm in a tiny plane, and, to top everything off, being wet and cold, had distracted her from her mission. Now all the pent-up anxiety flooded back.

"I bet he's in the bar," Maurice suggested. "It's by the pool we went past."

She nodded, unsure whether she'd be able to make it as far as the bar with legs that suddenly felt like pudding.

Maurice opened the door, switched on a light, and ushered her in with a flourish.

"Should I put your bags in the master suite?"

"No. My husband might be asleep up there."

She gave Maurice a generous tip, then locked the door behind him and leaned back against it. The tropical air had warmed her, but she needed to brush her hair, fix her make-up and pull herself together. However she needed to know whether Jake was in the bungalow even more, so she went down the hall to the living room that ran across the ocean side of the building. A wall of windows opened on a vista of creamy-white beach, night-blue water, and deep-purple sky.

Drawn to the gorgeous panorama, she walked to the sliding glass doors. Two people were strolling across the beach toward the main building, arms wrapped around each other's waists.

When they reached the walkway, the glow of the torches lit the woman's face.

Madison's world split open. Astrid – and Jake.

Chapter Eleven

Pain left Madison frozen and mute, but nothing she could have done or said would undo what she'd seen anyway.

Slowly the sharp edge of reality cut through the fog. She wanted to run after them, to yell and scream and demand that Jake never touch Astrid, or any other woman.

To demand that Jake love her.

She shook the impulse off with an effort. She refused to turn into her mother.

Maybe there was a good explanation as to why her husband's arm was around another woman's waist. Maybe Jake was helping his trusted employee, who'd no doubt had too much to drink, back to her room.

Astrid didn't seem the type to ever have more than one drink, but Madison was deep enough in denial to push the thought away.

When the pair disappeared into the maze of bungalows, she rested her forehead on the glass and let the tears flow.

Once the tremors of grief had passed, she straightened.

She came here because she'd decided Jake deserved a chance to explain. She intended to give him that chance, even if he did have more to explain. Once he got to the bungalow, they'd talk the whole the situation through like nice, sensible adults.

She turned on one of the Tiffany lamps by the sofa.

Jake would take a while to get Astrid to her room in her condition, so Madison showered, fixed her hair, did her best to conceal the ravages of her tears with make-up, and put on the black lace camisole and matching thong she'd bought. A small concession, but she refused to wear the flimsy garment where anyone but Jake was able to see. The matching black silk robe felt strangely cold against the bare skin the thong failed to cover.

She managed to eat an apple and an orange from the fruit basket on the bar, unsure how to fill the time. She had a few chapters left to read in her novel, but the story of other people's romantic woes was more than she wanted to deal with. She settled for an old movie on the huge plasma screen TV over the fireplace.

She checked the time. Eight-thirty. Jake must have stopped at the bar. He'd be here eventually and they could work things out. All Madison needed to do was wait.

She fell asleep on the sofa about two a.m., still waiting.

Jake's stomach was on fire and his mouth tasted of petroleum sludge. Apparently two mojitos, a couple of shots of tequila, and who knew how much whiskey possessed strange alchemical properties that condemned a man to living torment.

An ill-considered attempt to open his eyes spread the torment to his head. Tiny demons drummed on his temples while a larger one held his forehead in a vise which tightened at the slightest movement. With an effort, he allowed light to slash through what remained of his brain and lifted his head to look around. The room swooped in a circle and the fire in his belly came halfway up his throat before he managed to swallow the flaming bile.

He closed his eyes, reluctant to think the obvious "Where am I?"

His memories of the night before were dim, but the glance he'd gotten of the room didn't ring any bells. Maybe he'd managed to drag himself upstairs to the bungalow's master suite.

When someone knocked on a door, the sound pounded nails through his scalp. Never again, he vowed as every muscle tensed against the acoustic onslaught.

A murmur of voices, one male and an islander judging by the rhythm of it, the other female.

Madison! She'd come after all. He smiled with relief, forgetting for a moment the gritty toll of last night's binge. Until he tried to stand up and the world spun. He moaned and fell back, mouth clenched as he swallowed the fire rising up in his gullet.

"You're awake," said the female voice. "Or should I say conscious?"

Astrid. He fell into a deeper fiery pit, mental torment added to the physical torture.

Why was Astrid in his bungalow?

He blinked and groaned at the painful flash of light and the more painful truth it revealed.

She wasn't in his bungalow. He was on the couch in her room in the main building.

"Want some hair of the dog?" she asked.

He moved his head slowly side to side, mindful of the demons and their tools of torture.

If only he could remember what he did, or had tried to do, the night before. Maybe the clouds in his brain would fade after he got over the immediate effects of his efforts to drown his sorrows.

He thanked his lucky stars Madison was in San Francisco. Now he was grateful she'd overreacted. Whatever he'd done in his alcohol haze, he'd be able to work it out with his own conscience. She need never know.

The smell of coffee under his nose encouraged him to open his eyes again.

Bad idea. The light burned his brain and Astrid's amused grin reminded him he had more than one reason to worry about his actions the night before.

If he half-closed his eyes, he could almost form a coherent sentence.

"I didn't do or, er, try anything last night that might result in a lawsuit, did I?"

Astrid raised an eyebrow. "You still have all your important body parts?"

He wasn't entirely sure, but he nodded.

"Then you must not have. Mostly you ranted about your wife and passed out."

"What'd I say?"

"A bunch of nonsense about love and trust. Here, drink this." Astrid handed him a mug of coffee. "Either it'll clear your head, or you'll get the nasty stuff out of your stomach."

Odds were the result would be the second of those – which he richly deserved – but he took a sip of the dark, hot liquid anyway.

Despite the "do not disturb" sign on the bungalow's door, a house-keeping cart clattered across the walkway and woke Madison before it rattled off. She unfolded herself slowly from the sofa and glanced at the clock. Ten a.m.

Outside the glass doors the sun shone. The sparsely populated beach and the turquoise sea beckoned. Inside, all was dark and quiet. No sign of Jake.

Maybe he'd snuck past her last night after the bar closed, so he wouldn't wake her.

She crept up the staircase to the master suite. Her suitcase lay open where she'd left it on the bed. She closed her eyes against the threat of pain and went back downstairs to check the two smaller bedrooms. Both empty and untouched.

Her brain throbbed – no, no, no.

She looked out over the beach, dotted with brightly colored umbrellas. A scattering of vacationers lay in the sun or splashed in the surf. Two people appeared from the direction of the main building, a man and a woman, both in swimsuits, headed toward the ocean. A tall man and a short, dark woman.

The woman turned her head.

Astrid – and Jake. Again.

Madison's heart froze. All the clues, all the signs, all the lies she'd told herself the night before – probably the same lies her mother told herself for years – shifted and settled into an all-too-clear picture that burned in Madison's chest where her heart used to be.

One thought was clear in her brain. She needed to get away from here, away from the proof her marriage wasn't, had never been, anything but some sort of twisted game.

She was up the stairs in an instant. She literally tore the flimsy nightclothes off her body and stuffed them in her bag. She'd have thrown them in the trash, but she didn't want Jake to find out she'd been fool enough to buy the damned thong.

She showered off the remaining bits of hope, put on a clean pair of designer jeans and a black t-shirt, threw the rest of her clothes and cosmetics in the bag, and dashed down the stairs as if the devil himself might catch her. Or, worse, Jake.

She ran down the walkway, through the reception area, and out to the street to search frantically for a taxi. The same man who'd driven her there the night before was dozing in his battered cab. She knocked on the roof of the cab and he started awake.

"Can you drive me to the airport?"

"Lady, I just bring you from the airport last night."

"Yes, I remember. Can you take me back right now?"

He shrugged and opened the door for her.

"You crazy, you know that?"

"I'm paying you for a ride, not a diagnosis."

As they drove out of town, her insides twisted with the pain, leaving her as oblivious to the beauty around her as she was to the bumpy ride.

Once the driver dropped her at the small airport, she filled her mind with the dozens of transactions and explanations needed to buy a ticket on the next plane to Miami, which boarded in thirty minutes.

Only when she sat in regal solitude in the tiny first-class cabin, watching the island shrink into nothingness in the bright-blue

Caribbean, did the pain plunge her into despair.

Damn.

The romance novel, the glass, and the half-empty bottle of Perrier on the table by the sofa told Jake Madison she had been here. But where was she now?

He went upstairs, pulled off the wet trunks he'd bought an hour before in the resort shop, and dropped them on the bathroom floor as he dried the salt water out of his hair.

The dent in the duvet on the bed where she'd laid her suitcase gave him his answer. She was on her way home.

There were three flights a day to Miami. If she'd missed the first one, he could still catch her at the airport before she left. He showered and dressed in record time.

"Astrid," he said once she answered her phone, "I've got to leave right away. You go ahead and finish up the deal to buy this place. I can sign the papers later."

"What's wrong?"

"Madison was here last night."

"And you weren't." Astrid's tone was somewhere between amusement and sympathy.

"I might be able to stop her at the airport, if I hurry." He threw clothes into his bag with his free hand.

"I'll come with you," Astrid offered.

"No. We're in the middle of a major deal here." He moved into the bathroom and started clearing out his toiletries.

"I won't let you drive to the airport alone in the state you're in."

"How do you know what kind of state I'm in?"

"I know you love your wife. I'll meet you in the lobby."

He hung up. He didn't have the time to argue. If Astrid wasn't ready to leave the minute he was, he wasn't about to wait. He needed to find his wife and explain, before he lost the woman he loved for good.

At the airport, he jumped out of the rental car and sent Astrid back to the resort to finalize the deal. Not because he gave a damn about the resort anymore, but because he wanted time alone to figure out how to save his marriage.

He should have cancelled this trip as soon as he saw the note from Madison. And he should never have gotten so drunk last night.

He had to make Madison believe nothing had happened. A life without Madison was unthinkable.

He got through security just in time to watch her plane take off. Undeterred, he made the most of the perks of being very rich and began making phone calls.

The Carlyle & Sons' jet landed in the Bay Area slightly before sundown. Jake hopped off as soon as it rolled to a stop. He rushed through a cursory customs inspection to his waiting limo and mentally urged the Rolls through the snarl of the traffic with the drive and energy of a man on a mission.

When a red light and the threat of gridlock on the Embarcadero stalled the limo's forward progress, he jumped out and all but ran the rest of the way to his building.

The snail's pace of the elevator made him drum the sleek steel walls impatiently with his palms. As soon as the doors slid open, he burst past them, keys in hand, and let himself into the penthouse.

Madison jumped up from the piano bench with a gasp while the last chord she'd played still echoed in the air. He started toward her, but the tortured expression on her face stopped him.

He couldn't move, could scarcely breathe.

Her voice seemed to come from very far away as she said words he took a second or two to grasp.

"You cheated on me, you bastard. Just like my father."

She might as well have slapped him.

"I didn't."

"Don't make it worse by lying." Her hollow tone matched the emptiness in her eyes as she looked at him. "I was at the resort, Jake. I saw you walk to the hotel with her last night and down to the beach with her this morning."

148

"But you don't understand. . ."

"I understand plenty. I know more about unfaithful husbands than any woman should have to. But maybe you don't consider it infidelity. One of the advantages of a trophy wife is how easily she can be replaced with a shinier new trophy when the one you have becomes inconvenient, or you get tired of her. I flatter myself that you weren't tired of me yet."

Anger and hurt roared like a screaming jet in his head. "Let me explain."

She sat down again at the piano. "There's only one explanation for what you did. You're a cheater. It's natural, I guess, to be attracted to someone like my father."

"I am nothing like your father!"

"Don't you shout at me."

He nodded a silent apology.

"You've always known infidelity was the one thing I'd never be able to live with." She sounded as old and sad as time itself. "You should have thrown me out of your office the first time I showed up there and spared us both the heartache. Or at least you should have told me the truth and given me the choice." She swallowed. "You should have been honest enough to tell me you don't love me."

"But I. . ." He stopped before he said too much, the roaring in his ears louder than ever.

He refused to be like *his* father, either.

She ignored his protest, in any case. "If you can find another place to stay tonight, I'll be moved out of here by the end of the day tomorrow."

The pain was a torment of flashing red light in his head. He needed to go somewhere he could get a grip on his chaotic emotions and think. Afraid any words he found now would make the situation worse, he turned and walked out the door.

Madison sat in the resounding silence for a long time before she began to play the *Mephisto Waltz*. She'd miss the piano.

The thought stopped her mid-phrase, the music suddenly an unbearable symbol of all she'd lost. She stood with jerky, awkward movements, her body shaking.

Mrs. Lee appeared in the doorway, jacket in her hand.

"Did I hear Mr. Carlyle?"

Madison kept her voice even. "Yes, but he forgot some important papers at the office."

The lie came easily. An unfaithful husband was bad enough. She'd keep her anguish private. Her mother had taught her by example how to cover up a man's infidelities.

"Do you want anything before I leave?"

I want my husband back. My world back. "No, thank you. I'll see you tomorrow."

Madison waited, one hand on the piano to steady her, until she heard the service door close. Then she crumbled to the floor like an empty balloon.

Jake hesitated in front of the familiar door, unsure of his welcome. But a tiny movement at the window meant someone had heard his approach. Trapped, he rang the bell.

The housekeeper answered and led him out to the deck.

His mother didn't look surprised to see the son who was supposed to be in the Caribbean, so he skipped the pleasantries.

"Did Madison call you?"

"No. Tyler Ellsworth called to ask if I knew why his niece was in her office at Dartmoor headquarters instead of off on a vacation with you. Seems her COO called him. Cochrane, is it? In any case, they're both worried she's working too hard."

Jake lowered himself into a chair and watched the brown water from the Sacramento River fan out across the blue of the Bay in eternal pursuit of the receding Pacific Ocean tide.

"She's pretty busy with the Dartmoor updates," he said.

"Funny. I assumed you'd had a fight."

"I walked out on her two days ago." The lie burned. "No. She threw me out. Madison's left me." He swallowed the sharp-edged "again."

His mother closed her eyes. "I was afraid of that. Is it over?"

"I don't know."

"Do you want to talk about it?"

He shrugged. "I must, or I wouldn't be here."

"You might have come home for three hots and a cot."

He almost smiled. "What on earth have you been reading?"

"I heard it on television the other night."

"Madison. . ." Her name choked him, but he covered it with an empty laugh. "Madison and I have a pre-nup. I can afford a hotel, but she's moved back into her mother's apartment."

"Exactly what happened?" His mother finally turned toward him. "It'll take a while for Marisol to stretch dinner to feed two, in any case. I'm eager to hear how much of an idiot you've been this time."

Her certainty the mess was his fault pushed him to recount the story as calmly and honestly as he could. The part where Madison accused him of being like her father brought anger bubbling to the surface, until he remembered he'd insisted she skip graduate school and be a stay-at-home wife like his mother – and hers. He'd never told her why. The anger faded, leaving more room for pain. And self-reproach.

When he finished, his mother shivered in the cool breeze. He handed her the shawl she'd left on the chair where he was sitting.

"You are a bigger idiot than I suspected," she said.

"Thank you for your support." He kept his tone gentle.

"You didn't have to walk out. You could've stayed, explained, worked it out with her."

Jake stood and paced across the deck to stare down at the bay for a moment before he turned to face her.

"I shouldn't have to defend myself to Madison. I would never cheat on her. She should know that." His chest was so tight he could barely breathe, but he forged on. "I love her."

"Have you told her so?"

He sank back down in the chair, his thoughts too jumbled and painful for words.

When he remained silent, his mother said, "I have a story of my own, dear"

Something in her voice warned him he'd rather not hear this story, but he was apparently going to hear it anyway.

"It's a story about being afraid to tell the person you love that you love them."

His taut nerves tensed another notch.

"And this is relevant to me and Madison how?"

"I'll leave you to do the math, as they say. This story is about what me and your father."

"But you didn't. . ."

"Love your father? No, not at first, but he was a good man, and he adored me. Being adored changes a person, I think. Over the years, liking turned to fondness and fondness melted into love. But I never knew how to say the words." She turned to look out over the darkening water. "No, I never dared say the words, for fear of losing him."

"How can you lose someone by telling them you love them?"

She raised an eyebrow. "How indeed?"

He closed his eyes and the vulnerability washed over him, the need for Madison's love he'd refused to acknowledge, even to himself. In its wake came the sorrow he'd protected himself from, first by shutting her out of his life after she left him at the altar, then only letting her halfway back in by pretending their marriage was all about the Dartmoor mess.

But his insistence on marrying Madison had really been, had always been, about the immeasurable jolt of sheer joy he'd felt the day she walked into his office, as if everything missing from his life for three years rushed over him in one supreme wave of happiness.

He tried to map his situation onto his parents', but it couldn't make it fit.

As if she read his mind, his mother shook her head. "Your father was well aware from the start that I didn't love him. What if he loved me *because* I didn't love him? What if knowing I loved him changed his feelings about me? I wanted to confess, but the longer I waited, the easier it was to convince myself he'd hate me for not admitting it sooner. I was too much of a coward to risk it. And now it's too late."

"Suicidal depression is an illness," Jake reminded them both.

"Emotions don't care much about the facts."

They sat in silence until the deck lighting flickered on to draw a shimmering curtain against the fog rolling in below them.

After a few minutes, his mother added, "It would be easier to live with my mistakes if you learned from them."

"The situation's not the same," he protested. "You were afraid..."

His mother gave him a long look.

He was afraid, too. Not afraid that Madison would stop loving him if he confessed his love for her, exactly, but afraid of putting himself on the line when she might not feel as deeply about him as he did about her. After all, she'd left him at the first hint he might have cheated.

Okay, maybe it was more than a hint. Still, she hadn't let him explain. She'd assumed he was like her father, repeating the pattern of her parents' marriage the same way he feared repeating his parents'. He wanted to be the most important thing in her life. If he told her that and she chose Dartmoor over him, he might shatter completely.

Suddenly he heard his father's voice echoing words Madison had said what seemed like a very long time ago. "Could you sell Carlyle's?"

The tectonic plates of his life shifted into a new, very different, shape.

He'd asked her to make a choice he'd never have to make – between their relationship and her family's legacy. That was unfair.

More, it over-simplified the way life was. Madison was the most important thing in his life, but she wasn't the only important thing. What if that's how she'd felt about him? If he'd expected more from her than he was willing to give in return, maybe he'd been thinking of her as a trophy wife after all, as someone he owned, controlled. Surely there was some middle ground between that and the one-sided love that had slowly broken his father's heart, a place where they could meet as equal partners.

The possibility opened new vistas of hope. He had to find a way to talk to her, so he could convince her he was willing to find that place together. And, he acknowledged with a nod at his mother, so he could tell her how much he loved her.

He wasn't sure he had the courage. But a life without Madison...

An email subject line flashed into his mind. "Forensic audit results."

Unable to face anything associated with Dartmoor, he'd ignored the message from his accountant when it came in. But it might be the key to getting Madison to listen to him.

If Dana Ellsworth was surprised to come back from Sonoma and find Madison living in the apartment, she didn't show it.

"What's wrong?" was all she said when she saw her daughter's stony face.

"I left Jake." Madison swallowed the tears and pain as best she could. "He cheated on me with his PA."

Her mother raised her eyebrows. "Really? His PA? Even your father was generally more imaginative. And more sensitive to the potential for lawsuits."

Madison hadn't considered the legal aspect. But it didn't change what she'd seen.

Her mother asked the housekeeper to bring some brandy, then sat next to Madison on the sofa. "When did you find out about the PA?"

Madison blinked against a wave of new pain. "A few days ago."

"While you were in the Caribbean?"

Madison nodded and poured out the whole story.

"I was afraid this would happen," her mother said, then took a sip of brandy.

"Why? You were always fond of Jake."

"I am. But you married him in such a hurry. You should have spent more time together before you took such a big step."

"We'd spent plenty of time together. We'd almost gotten married before, remember?"

"But you didn't. Have you ever discussed what went wrong?"

Madison stared into her glass. "He understands why I didn't marry him the first time."

"But have you really talked about it?"

They'd talked, but only about the facts, not about the emotions behind them. "Sort of."

"And now you think you've ended up the way I did, stuck with a philandering husband."

"I know I have."

"Jake is nothing like your father. You know that, too."

"But Father. . ."

She stopped, stymied by the need to say so much that words couldn't describe – the sly looks from strangers when they went places where her father took his other women, the empty ache when he disappeared for days, the public humiliation when he died in his mistress's bed.

"Madison, he cheated on me, not you," her mother said gently

"I'm not sure it doesn't come to the same thing."

Besides, she wasn't ready to tell her mother the whole truth. The problem between her and Jake went much deeper than whether he cheated or not. Even if he had a good story about what happened that night, the fact remained that he'd invited her along on the trip as a convenience. CEO and Chair of the Dartmoor Board or not, that's what she was to him, a convenience, a trophy wife. Not a person he considered an equal, trusted – or loved.

Her mother gave herself a little shake and said, "Why didn't you call and tell me, dear?"

"I—I thought I could deal with it. I was okay for a while." She'd been numb, drained dry of tears, but "okay" was close enough. "Until I checked my calendar and saw an appointment with Jake's lawyer set for tomorrow afternoon. I assume it means he wants a divorce."

"Have you discussed divorce?"

Now for the hard part.

No, all of this was hard. Numb silence was better, but this new blow had jolted Madison out of her stupor, into unexpected levels of grief and regret.

"We haven't discussed anything. We haven't talked at all."

"He refuses to speak to you?"

"I refuse to speak to him. He even came here, but I didn't let him in."

"I can see how he might consider your marriage over."

"Mother, he cheated on me. How can I talk to him?"

Sudden embarrassment, for both of them, brought a wave of heat to her face. Her mother hadn't just spoken to her unfaithful husband, she'd lived with him, slept with him for years. Madison didn't have the heart to explain that was exactly why she'd avoided any contact with Jake, for fear he'd use her love for him to coerce her into the life she'd vowed she'd never accept.

"If you don't even want to speak to him, you should be happy about a divorce."

"What I am is confused. Up until yesterday, he wanted to talk to me."

"Maybe he thinks this will force you to talk to him."

Not a thought Madison dared to take seriously. "Sending his lawyer is a bit extreme."

"He might feel extreme measures are called for."

Madison didn't have anything to say on the subject, only questions. Did her husband resort to "extreme measures" because he

them off, the woman in a headscarf who worked in cosmetics asked if he'd seen the questionnaire in the foyer. The older man in handbags said, "No worries about the right size." The college-age woman in candy corrected herself – "Or for the man in your life."

Once he stepped off the elevator on the top floor, though, only silence greeted him. The hall seemed to stretch a very long way to the executive suite. The sound of his footsteps was muffled by the worn carpet as he walked by a hundred and fifty years of framed newspaper ads, but he was aware of every step taking him closer to his goal.

The cozy-looking the receptionist greeted him with another happy smile.

"I'm here to see. . ." Ms. Ellsworth or Mrs. Carlyle? His gut did a somersault. That was why he'd come, wasn't it? To find out. "Ms. Ellsworth."

When the receptionist didn't correct him, but clicked on the outdated computer on her desk, Jake's hands tightened into fists. He loosened them slowly, finger by finger.

"Mr. Gordon?" the receptionist asked.

"No. Gordon couldn't make it, so I came instead."

"Oh. Okay." She pushed a button on the old-fashioned intercom. "Ms. Ellsworth, your two o'clock appointment is here." She pointed him, not toward the office still labeled "Mr. Ellsworth," but down the hall past it.

This hall was far shorter than the one from the elevator to the receptionist's desk, but it felt twice as long. Each step took a conscious effort.

Finally he reached the half-open door at the end of the hall.

The room beyond it was dominated not by the desk, which was pushed into one corner, but by a circular antique table. The woman behind the desk lifted her head and the sunlight glinted off her soft blonde hair. He watched the emotions cross her face as she slowly stood – shock, anger, then a hint of fear before a mask settled into place. She gave him a twisted smile.

"I was expecting your lawyer." Her voice sounded twisted, too.

Surprise was about the only point in his favor, but he hated how white she'd gone.

"You'd have refused to meet with me."

She didn't say anything, but gestured at the chair opposite her at the desk and sank into hers. He'd have preferred to stand, but it wouldn't help his cause to loom over her, so he settled into the well-worn leather chair.

"Why the subterfuge?" Her voice was under control, but her eyes were still wide with surprise and something like panic.

"I have some highly confidential information to share with you that needs to be conveyed in person."

Her expression softened and she met his gaze for the first time. "Personal information?"

"Information about Dartmoor."

The mask slammed back into place. She looked away. "So, we're face to face. Tell me."

"Not here."

She straightened and steepled her hands in a gesture eerily reminiscent of her father.

"Why not? We're alone and you can be assured the office isn't bugged."

Because the building was still in the technological Stone Age, but he didn't dare say so.

"I said it was highly confidential. Once I explain, you'll understand why we can only discuss it where we can be completely alone."

She raised an eyebrow. "Your bed, perhaps?"

He exploded out of his chair, crossed the room, and came back to loom over her after all.

"Damn it, Madison, I'm serious. If I wanted you in my bed. . ."

All the strategies for seducing his wife he'd thought up over the last week replayed through his brain in a rush of erotic images that rendered him momentarily speechless.

But then he noticed how the mask she wore seemed to have

cracked and left pieces of different expressions on her face – pain in her tight lips, pride in her lifted chin, grief in her eyes.

"I'm sorry." She cleared her throat. "I shouldn't have jumped to conclusions."

He'd said, "If. . ." Damn. He couldn't remember a time he didn't want her in his bed.

But this wasn't the time to tell her so. He'd make up for the lapse later.

"Should I come to your office?" The professional calm of her voice jarred against the shards of emotion on her face.

"No. It's not any more private there. It'll have to be at our. . . the penthouse. This evening." Her gaze had iced over, pushing his carefully rehearsed words out awkwardly, like a teenager asking a girl to the prom. "I'll have Mrs. Lee leave us dinner."

"No need. I won't be there long."

The way her suit hung loose on her body suggested she needed a good meal, but all he said was, "Whatever. Just show up. This is important, Madi."

He sat down again and waited. He'd cut enough deals to know the drill. No matter what he said at this point, it was liable to provoke an objection. If he let the silence stretch out, odds were she'd say something to break it. "Yes" would be easiest. Or "No."

But apparently she'd learned a bit about negotiation in business school herself.

"Can you tell me what kind of information you have?"

"It has to do with Dartmoor's financial situation."

Her eyes opened in surprise. "That's one kind I really can't ignore, isn't it? What time?"

"Six?"

"Okay." The word sounded tortured out of her.

They both stood at the same moment and stared at each other across her cluttered desk.

"Madi. . ." Her name came out rough with longing. He swallowed. "I'll see you then."

161

On the interminable elevator ride to the penthouse, Madison was able to lean against the side of the metal cubicle, but couldn't gauge whether she'd be able to stand, not to mention walk, on her unsteady legs once she reached the top.

Her empty stomach growled. Maybe she shouldn't have turned down Jake's offer of dinner. She would be there a while, after all. Her mother was right – they needed to talk about far more than whatever Jake had learned about Dartmoor.

Her mind skittered away from the reality waiting for her on the top floor.

Instead she scanned her reflection in the sleek steel wall opposite her. She'd been weak enough to stop by the apartment to change into a suit that still fit: a dark-green one she'd bought soon after her father's death, when she'd got tired of black. The color muted the green of her eyes, but she already knew seduction wasn't on Jake's agenda for tonight.

She wished like hell his dismissive comment didn't hurt so much, but the pain was permanently lodged in her chest, just under the battered remains of her heart.

The elevator lurched to such an abrupt halt she was thankful for an empty stomach. As the doors slid open, she pushed away from the wall and found a balance between the quivering of her body and her determination not to let Jake know he'd reduced her to a pile of nerves.

One step across the small but elegant foyer, two, three. . .

The door to the penthouse was ajar.

She'd left her key on the dining table the day she moved out, but Jake had arranged it so she didn't need to ring the bell of her former home. She tried not to read too much into his thoughtfulness. Hesitantly she knocked.

"Come in."

Out of habit, she laid her purse in the usual place on the hall table before she stepped into the living area. The sight of the piano – her piano – made her eyes sting, but she looked past it to Jake, who was setting a platter of tapas by a bowl of gardenias on the coffee table.

"You said you didn't want dinner, but. . ."

"Thank you."

They stared at each other the same way they had in her office earlier, but the air between them, merely heavy in the less intimate space, was now leaden with tension, hot with emotion.

He gestured toward the sofa. "Please have a seat. Would you like some wine?"

"Y-yes, please." She lowered herself onto the black leather and noticed the tablet computer next to the flower bowl. "But only half a glass. This is a business meeting, after all."

He gave a non-committal noise and took a bottle of Cabernet from the dining table.

The fire was lit, but turned down low. The vase her employees had given them for a wedding gift sat on the mantel with three roses in it – red, white, and pink. Beyond the windows, fog hid the ocean side of the City, but the Bay side was the usual dazzle of lights.

She tried one of the tapas, but was too nervous to notice how it tasted.

Jake handed her a glass, careful their fingers didn't touch, then sat several feet away on the sofa and picked up the tablet.

"After I first saw the financials for Dartmoor, I sent them out for a forensic audit."

"No!" Panic squeezed her lungs. "I told you I'd – we'd decided against that. The cost. . ."

Not that money was the real reason for her alarm.

"I paid for it personally."

"But why?"

"Because something felt off to me, but I didn't have the technical expertise to figure out what it was. I don't like mysteries when it comes to business, especially financial mysteries."

Her uneasy stomach went into full revolt. No wonder he hadn't wanted to tell her this at the office. Her father. . .

"The audit didn't find any smoking guns."

She let out a slow breath and sank back on the cushions.

"What they did find were questionable reimbursements for expenditures at luxury boutiques, furriers, restaurants, and casinos in Las Vegas and elsewhere. All fully documented and spread over the entire four years your father's mistress was CFO of Dartmoor, so no one incident stood out. But a few hundred thousand here, a few hundred thousand there adds up. Taken together it's enough to turn the evidence over to the District Attorney."

Madison gasped. "You didn't. That woman will drag. . ."

"Precisely why I brought the information to you before I approached the DA. I'm fairly certain your ex-CFO can be persuaded to repay Dartmoor for the dubious expenditures rather than run the risk of criminal charges. After all, once the audit goes to the DA, even if he chooses not to prosecute, the information might leak out to the press." He smiled a not very nice smile. "And what would become of her shiny new career at that hedge fund?"

"How much money are we talking about?" Not that it mattered. Confronting her father's mistress with evidence that could ruin her would be its own reward.

"Enough to finance the renovations to the first floor of your flagship store."

Madison took a gulp of her wine. The flagship store was the key to the success of her whole plan, but the age of the building made getting bank loans for the changes there beyond difficult. If they didn't have to rely on outside capital, they could put it next on the list for renovations. Her mind whirled with the possibilities.

Jake pushed the platter closer to her. "More tapas?"

"No. Yes. I mean, no. I have to thank you first. Oh, thank you, Jake. This is everything I wanted. I can't wait to share the news with everyone at Dartmoor."

"You'll need to figure out just what to tell them, but I'm glad it worked out this way."

A long silence sucked the air out of the room.

They reached for tapas at the same moment. Their fingers touched. Electricity arced through the air as they both jerked their hands back.

"W-was that all you had to discuss?" She took another swallow of wine.

"No."

Fear and something like hope battled over the remnants of her heart.

"You left me at the damn altar, Madi."

She blinked in surprise. "What choice did I have after what I heard you say?"

He gave a low laugh. "I should never have lied to you about that. You know what I really said to Mark? I told him you were the ultimate trophy wife because I loved you. I still love you."

Her heart stopped for a moment, but she refused to surrender to the joy too easily.

"If you loved me. . ."

"I should have wanted you to do what would make you happy. I see that now, but I was only twenty-four and. . ." He closed his eyes, leaned his head back, and ran his hand through his hair. "Madi, my father jumped off that damned boat. Right smack in the middle of the Bay."

She laid one hand on his knee, surprised when he allowed it.

Jake sighed. "He'd been depressed for years, but it got worse and worse."

"I had no idea."

So many things made sense now that hadn't before.

"We couldn't let anyone know."

"Including my father," she acknowledged. "I wouldn't have told him."

"I couldn't be sure of that. Which meant that, by the time we were supposed to get married the first time, I was running a billion-dollar corporation with an MBA and virtually no experience, while trying to keep my father's illness a secret." He sat up and took her hand in his. "It's because I've been there that I'm so impressed with what you've done for Dartmoor."

Impressed? A honeyed warmth spread through her.

"I have a lot of help."

"I needed your support. I needed you to be there for me full-time." He lifted her hand and kissed it.

"If I'd known, I'd have put off business school."

He gave a low, harsh laugh. "I was planning to tell you everything on our honeymoon."

"Oh, Jake, I'm so sorry." She blinked back tears.

"It's water under the bridge. I've learned I don't have to be jealous of Dartmoor."

She was so startled she almost pulled her hand away. "Jealous?"

"I needed you so much back then, but you seemed more devoted your career there than you were to me."

She knew him well enough to understand the fear behind his words. He'd been afraid of loving her more than she loved him, of repeating his father's sad story.

His hand shook slightly as he caressed her palm. "The important thing is that you're here beside me now."

She wanted to tell him he could have her by his side forever, but then reality hit her like a bucket of ice water. "But you and Astrid. . ."

He freed her hand and groaned. She rushed on before he could tell her the truth she wasn't ready, would never be ready to hear.

"It's probably my fault. I pushed you into it when I said I wasn't coming to the island."

"That's not much of an excuse."

"No, but I've thought about it a lot. . ." She forced herself to breathe against the pain, each word etched into her heart. "And i–it's okay."

"Really?" His voice was tight. "Since you left me over it, I assumed you cared whether I slept with Astrid or not."

"Cared?" Surprise knocked the truth out of her. "It nearly killed me."

Her words hung in the air between them for a moment before he leaned forward, elbows on his knees, gaze fixed on the Berber carpet.

"The fact of the matter is. . ."

She focused on the hands knotted in her lap, unable to look at him.

"I spent the night passed out on Astrid's sofa."

Madison let out a long breath she hadn't been aware she was holding.

"It's nice to know nothing happened, even if you wanted. . ." Her voice wobbled.

"I did *not* want. I wasn't sure it was safe for her to walk back to the hotel after dinner alone. We stopped at the bar on the way, and I got so drunk I passed out in her room instead of in the bungalow."

"Oh." Madison ignored a rush of relief, determined to make a full confession, no matter how painful. "But you need to know that I decided that. . . that if you loved me enough to work on our marriage, I'd forgive you for cheating. Once."

He chuckled at her emphasis on the final word, then sobered. "But your father. . ."

"Because of my father. You are not him, and you're not your father, either. Just like I'm not either of our mothers. We're who we are, with our own choices to make, our own lives to live. We don't have to repeat the past."

"Damn it, Madi, how could I ever want anyone else when I have you?"

Those words, more than the declaration of love she hadn't let herself believe, brought all the broken pieces of her heart back to life and bound them together again into something whole and real, stronger than before. She drew her first full breath since she'd left him that awful note.

He took her hand in his and lifted it to his lips, his thumb fondling the rings she still wore. "Come live with me and be my love, Madi."

"Yes." She threw her arms around him with enough force to topple them both over on the sofa, but neither minded as lips met lips, flesh met flesh, heart met heart.

Only the awkwardness of their position pulled them reluctantly back to earth.

Jake stood to throw his crumpled jacket on the chair, undid his tie, and helped Madison to her feet, a procedure made more difficult because she's lost a shoe under the sofa. Finally she kicked the other one after it and found herself swept up into his arms.

"I have a little surprise for you."

He carried her into the bedroom and set her on the floor. The room they'd shared had been transformed into a floral paradise. A vase holding a single gardenia sat on her dresser. A path of white rose petals led to the bathroom and a path of pink ones from there to the bed, which was covered with piles of red rose petals.

"It's lovely, but why?"

"I wanted everything to be special, perfect for you tonight."

Speechless with emotion, she rose on tiptoes to kiss his cheek.

"I suspected you might not be ready for us to, er, have our reunion right away, so I thought maybe a bath first sounded like a good idea." He gestured to the rose petal paths.

"Thank you." She looked away. "But I have to ask – what would you have done if I'd said our marriage was over?"

He grimaced. "I'd have closed off these rooms and never come into them again. I've slept in the guest room every night since you left, as it is."

"Oh, Jake." She threw her arms around his neck and kissed him long and hard.

Very slowly, he pulled out of her embrace.

"Bath?"

She wasn't sure it was a question, but he'd gone to so much

trouble. . . She licked her lips and gave him a lascivious smile before she reached up to undo the buttons on her jacket.

He moaned. "Maybe it's better if I don't watch you undress. I'll wait in there."

He kicked off his shoes and winked at her as he slipped into the bathroom.

She finished undressing, then followed the path of rose petals and knocked on the bathroom door. He opened it completely, as gloriously naked as she was, and bowed her in.

The marble floor of the room was strewn with rose petals in all shades, from deepest red to palest pink. More petals floated in the tub. Their aroma mixed with the luxuriant scent of the gardenia to create an atmosphere more intoxicating than any wine.

Almost reverently Jake ran his gaze over her body, heating her everywhere he looked, while she stared her fill at him. Yet it was the tenderness in his eyes that undid her.

She blinked back tears and stepped into the tub amid the floating rose petals. Only when she was covered to her neck with water and roses did Jake lower himself into the other end of the tub, his feet alongside her hips, hers tucked between his thighs.

He gave her a lop-sided grin. "I'm not sure how well this part will work, but try not to laugh if it backfires, okay?"

Which made her laugh, of course.

"I asked you not to laugh."

"You asked me to try. Besides, it hasn't backfired yet."

"Yes, it has. You laughed."

The sulky expression on his face was contradicted by the teasing gleam in his eyes.

"Laughter is good," she told him.

He reached over and turned on the spa jets. She had visions of rose petals flying everywhere, and clearly he did, too, but the bubbly water merely bounced the bits of pink and red around so their rich perfume was more intense. A few petals stuck to his chest, her shoulders.

"Nice." Her eyelids fell shut.

He brushed a stray petal off her neck, just below the ear, and stroked both hands slowly from her hips to her ankles. "Nice."

The water did nothing to cool the flames that flowed from his fingers down her legs and spread upward to ignite the heat in her core until she was too boneless with pleasure to move.

Casually he rubbed her ankles to release all the day's tension and add fuel to the flames in her core. She gave a deep sigh of release and he lifted one foot to kiss the sensitive arch.

Her eyes popped open in time to see him smile at her gasp of surprised delight.

He wiggled his eyebrows, flicked a rose petal off one of her nipples, and lathered his hands to wash and caress her breasts until her head fell back with a moan.

When he finally rested his hand on her knees, she stirred herself to sitting and reached for the soap. He tensed slightly, but offered no protest when she used it to wash his already hardened flesh, stroking and teasing until he stopped her hands with his.

"The water's cooling off." He swallowed. "Why don't we move this to the bed?"

When she nodded, he got out of the tub and wrapped a red towel around his waist. He held her hand as she stepped onto the marble floor and enveloped her in a heated pink one. With a lazy smile he drew the soft cloth across her body, half to dry her, half to arouse her even more.

She gave a low moan when he massaged her backside with the rough cloth in a way that tugged gently at her heated core. He chuckled and kissed her belly as he knelt to dry her feet. Finally he pulled the towel away to dry the wet ends of her hair, leaving her naked.

After he hung her towel on the rack, she took his and dried him as he had her, except she planted her kiss, not on his belly, but on the silky tip of his desire.

He groaned and swept her up in his arms to carry her into the

170

bedroom and drop her on the rose-covered bed. The sensuous feel of the petals under her body, the heady perfume of the flowers filled her eyes with sentimental tears, her body with yearning.

He lowered the lights and lay next to her. She eagerly edged closer to kiss the soft skin along his shoulders, nibble at his neck, nip gently at his ears. Bold now, she shifted so she could run her fingernails lightly across his chest.

With a moan, he captured both of her hands in one of his to hold her still while he stroked her, shoulder to hip, in delicate tantalizing sweeps rich with the promise of more to come.

When she lifted her head to kiss him again, he released her hand to gather her breasts in his, then dipped his head to lick the already hardened nipples.

She urged her body against his and he slid his touch to her core, stroking the sensitive flesh until she let the climax crash through her as she writhed under him.

As she settled back to reality, he rained kisses across her cheeks.

"I've missed you so much, Madi. Please say you'll never leave me again."

"Why would I? You're everything I've ever wanted."

"And you're everything I'll ever need."

She reached down to stroke the hard shaft pressed into her belly. "Speaking of needs. . ."

He gave a low laugh before he kissed her solemnly and began to make love to her again with a gentle passion that sent them both far above the clouds, soaring together toward perfect pleasure in a shower of the colored stars of endless love.

Acknowledgements

Many thanks, first of all, to my agent, Scott Eagan, and my editor, Charlotte Ledger, for seeing through my words to the far better story this turned out to be.

I could never have done this without my amazing critique partners -- Ellen Lindseth, Lizbeth Selvig, and Laramie Sasseville (who writes as Naomi Stone). In addition to making me a better writer, they keep me going through the dark times and are always there to make the good times better.

I'd also like to express my appreciation to the members of Midwest Fiction Writers for many years of friendship and mentorship, and to the Romance Writers of America, whose contests (including the Golden Heart™) helped me hone my craft and get my writing out into the world.

Finally, endless love to my wonderful husband and our two children, who put up with bad moods, missed meals, and general lack of attention for far too long waiting for this to happen.